LARGE TYPE NUELLE

Nuelle, Helen.

The treacherous heart
    $5.95

THE TREACHEROUS HEART

Helen Nuelle

Kimberly Cartwright reveled in the riverscape near her home – the blue skies, the cool water, the tiny islands dotting the Mississippi. Kim was determined to help her father keep the family marina afloat but found herself swept up in a storm of conflicting emotions. Christopher Hawke, a brash young yachtsman, had a reputation for getting what he wanted. Did he want Kim or the marina? Was she about to set sail on waves of happiness or would he lead her into the treacherous shoals of heartbreak and despair?

Other Large Print Books
by Helen Nuelle

THE LONG ENCHANTMENT

THE TREACHEROUS HEART

Helen Nuelle

Curley Publishing, Inc.
South Yarmouth, Ma.

Library of Congress Cataloging-in-Publication Data

Nuelle, Helen.
   The treacherous heart / Helen Nuelle.—Large print ed.
      p.   cm.
   1. Large type books.   I. Title.
   [PS3564.U34T74   1990]
   813′.54—dc20
   ISBN 0–7927–0525–4 (hard: lg. print)   90–32039
   ISBN 0–7927–0526–2 (soft: lg. print)   CIP

Published in Large Print by arrangement with Donald MacCampbell, Inc. in the United States, Canada, the U.K. and British Commonwealth.

Distributed in Great Britain, Ireland and the Commonwealth by CHIVERS LIBRARY SERVICES LIMITED, Bath BA1 3HB, England.

Printed in Great Britain

THE TREACHEROUS HEART

CHAPTER 1

Just after dawn Kimberly Cartwright drove into the marina parking lot, turned off the engine, and sat silently regarding the scene before her.

Perhaps it was her own mood, she thought, but the place looked even more seedy and run-down than usual. The peeling paint and loose boards on the floating docks had been there yesterday, as had the weeds in the white gravel driveway and the collection of broken anchors, propeller blades, and folding-chair frames against the side wall of the dry dock. Nothing had changed except her own outlook. Suddenly she was tired – tired, disgusted, and discouraged. For three years she had struggled to keep the marina operational, slaved long hard hours, pinched pennies wherever she could, without asking – even of herself – why she bothered, when her father undermined all her efforts with his persistent drinking and gambling.

Once, the marina that Richard Cartwright had built from a tiny, one-dock landing to a flourishing enterprise had been his whole life. But when Kimberly's mother had died three years before, something vital had gone out of him, and Kimberly, who had come home from college for the funeral, found herself staying home in the little village of Elsah, Illinois, for weeks that finally lengthened into months and then dragged into years. It had been no hardship at first, for she loved the tiny old village. She gloried in the ever-changing panorama of sky, water, and towering bluffs above Alton Dam, where the Mississippi River broadened into the long, wide stretch of Alton Lake, dotted with islands and busy with pleasure craft. But now, with money so scarce that she had found it necessary to let almost half of the help at the marina go, the charm had vanished. Only last week she had regretfully told the painter that she could no longer afford his services, and so she was now here at this ungodly hour, intending to try her own hand at painting a motor sailer.

It was a small boat and she hadn't expected painting it to be difficult, but it had already taken her two whole days, barring the many interruptions, merely to mask the brightwork and the green trim. She had gone home tired and discouraged the evening before, only to find her father gone. This morning he still had not returned. Even a year ago an absence of that duration would have sent her into a panic, but it happened so often now that she

2

had ceased to worry about him. Nevertheless, a small kernel of concern would stay with her until she knew he was safe.

Normally Kimberly would have gloried in a spring morning such as this, but now she glanced sourly down the length of the lake, where the rising sun was painting the water a crinkled gold. Behind her, on the other side of the River Road, the towering bluffs were splashed with the same brilliance, the deep curves and scallops, worn by thousands of years of wind and water, shadowed from mauve to dark purple. The brush and trees on their lower slopes still retained the fresh green of spring, but this morning their charm had fled.

"Morning, Miss Cartwright."

Having just stepped out of the car, she turned to greet the night watchman, catching his quick glance at her disreputable appearance. Besides the old bandanna tied around her hair she wore a pair of ragged blue jeans and a T-shirt whose original color was long lost in many washings.

"Good morning, Mr. Glass. Is everything all right?"

"Dull night. Not even any motorcycle kids on the road." Then, unable to curb his curiosity, he added, "You look like you're set to do some work."

3

"Yes, I'm going to paint that motor sailer in the paint shack."

His kind old face creased with doubt. "You could let one of the boys do it," he suggested. Kimberly read disapproval in his eyes that she knew was directed not at her but at her father.

"They have their own work," she told him quietly. "I can do this." But inwardly she was raging at Richard Cartwright for causing her this embarrassment, and the angry resentment that had begun to wane was back again as she turned to the car, avoiding Mr. Glass's eyes as she lifted out the clothing she would wear when she finished painting.

Leaving her clothing in the marine store at the edge of the parking lot, Kimberly hurried toward the steps that led down to the marina. It was a vaguely oval harbor dredged from the flatland along the edge of the river. The earth had been piled at its outer perimeter and now formed a curved finger of land that tapered to a point at the narrow waterway that was the entrance to the harbor. Roofed floating docks, connected to the land by planked footwalks, lined the edge of the harbor, their slips holding every variety of craft, from the smallest motorboat to Dr. Benning's sixty-foot cruiser, a yacht that bespoke unlimited wealth.

Kimberly sighed as she turned to her right

4

and walked down the graveled driveway toward the buildings beyond the harbor. It was a good marina, she thought, her sour mood beginning to dissipate. She would do everything she could to save it for her father, but sometimes it did seem hopeless. If only he would . . . But she brushed the thought away, decided to have another talk with him tonight, not mull over it during the day.

Two hours later Kimberly stood back from the half-painted motor sailer in despair. It just seemed to be one of those days that started badly and gradually became intolerable, for now the paint gun refused to work. It had sputtered, spurted, and threatened to choke while she was painting the sides of the craft and now it had clogged completely. She was tempted to dash it to the ground in a fit of temper. And it was not just this one day, she thought, but an accumulation of disappointments and frustrations that had been building since the beginning of the boating season five weeks ago. For the first time she admitted to herself that she could not keep the marina going with the paltry sum of money that was left after Richard Cartwright's gambling sprees. Sadly she gazed out the open door of the paint shack, looking down the length of the marina to the old side-wheel steamer

5

that was moored just within the finger of land near the entrance to the harbor. Richard Cartwright had bought it many years ago and it had long served as a profitable restaurant, but last year they had sold it. The money from this sale had seen the marina through the season. Even that had been accomplished only because Kimberly had taken most of the money and banked it in her own name.

As she stood musing somberly, a cruiser moved into the harbor, coming slowly into sight around the bulk of the side-wheeler. It was a luxurious yacht, not as large as Dr. Benning's, but at least forty feet long. Suddenly she remembered that this must be Dr. Benning's friend. Several weeks before, Benning had called, asking them to hold the slip next to his boat for a friend, who would be arriving at some indefinite time. That was the only slip large enough for a big cruiser. She liked yachts because they gave the marina a prosperous appearance.

Quickly Kimberly put down the fractious gun and removed the goggles that were standard wear for spray painters, ready to welcome the new arrival. Suddenly aware of herself, she glanced down in dismay. Her hands and arms were dripping with paint. The jeans – old and ragged at the best of times – now had a fine coating of white paint, as did

6

her canvas shoes. If she could have sneaked away to the marine store to clean up, she would have done so, but she would have had to walk the length of the marina to reach it, passing directly in front of the cruiser. Even if she went up the driveway to the parking level, she would still be seen crossing over to the store. It was not so much pride as business sense that caused her indecision; it was poor policy for the owner, and a girl at that, to be so obviously driven to doing work for which she should have hired help. It gave the marina a desperate, poverty-stricken public image. To avoid this image and conceal their hand-to-mouth existence, Kimberly always dressed well while working and usually, whenever she could, tried to appear to be more a hostess to their customers while keeping books and tending to the marine store in quiet hours.

Kimberly had almost reached the yacht and was thinking that if the owner stayed in the cabin, she would go on to the store and let him seek her out there, when he appeared on deck. Expecting to see another bald, paunchy version of Dr. Benning, she was startled for a moment and then quickly decided that this must be a crewman or navigator Christopher Hawke had hired to bring him down the Illinois River from Chicago. He had not yet seen her and Kimberly stood fascinated as

7

she watched him swing down the ladder with fluid grace. The controlled, athletic strength in his movements reminded her of the easy flow of muscles in a leopard, for the blue-and-white striped T-shirt that spanned his broad chest and shoulders fitted like skin. As he stepped onto the dock he turned and their eyes met, his black in a copper-tanned face. He had black hair too, which gleamed blue in the sunlight.

The black eyes swept from her bandanna-wrapped head to her paint-smeared shoes, and Kimberly came back to herself with a start, acutely aware of herself and as embarrassed at her appearance as if she stood there stark naked.

"I – I was painting," she said lamely as if that was not entirely evident.

A glint appeared in the black eyes, and the corners of his wide mouth twitched. It was a humorous mouth, clear-cut and well shaped, but at the moment he appeared to be trying to control it. Then Kimberly saw that his shoulders were shaking slightly, and she realized he was laughing at her. Her amber eyes flashed and narrowed as quick anger mounted in her, but the anger was as much at herself as at him, for he was probably some river bum, lazy, taking any job that was offered just to live on the river, and she, like

8

a fool, stood gawking at him because he was handsome. Not even really handsome, she thought, correcting herself; his features were too rugged.

"Do you find something amusing?" she asked coolly, her chin out and her head tilted at a haughty angle, prepared to put him in his place.

Her words appeared to be too much for his self-control, and he tossed back his head and frankly laughed out loud. Kimberly would have turned and walked away, but she refused to be defeated by him. She glowered angrily, unwilling to shout to be heard above the sound of his laughter; she would subdue him with condescending words and haughty dignity.

"I see nothing amusing," she said when the yelping laughter trailed into chuckles.

"No, you wouldn't. You lack the proper perspective." The black eyes were still glinting with amusement.

"From my perspective I see only ignorance and bad manners," she spat at him, forgetting to be dignified.

"But your perspective is very limited. Or perhaps it's your sense of humor that's lacking. Now, if we've finished insulting each other, tell me your name."

"My name is none of your business. I don't

9

associate with river bums, and the only reason I stopped was to talk to Mr. Hawke. You can tell him I'll be at the marine store." She turned quickly to leave, unwilling to bandy any more words with him. She had the distinct feeling that she was coming off second best in this exchange. Her own gawking interest when she first saw him had put her at a distinct disadvantage.

"I'll be glad to tell him and I'm certain he'll be there, but I think his business is with Mr. Cartwright, so can you tell me why you assume he will want to see you?" There was taunting laughter in his voice that Kimberly ignored as she moved away haughtily, her head held high.

At the paint shed she had wiped her hands and arms with rag. Now, going through the store, she picked up a can of turpentine on her way to the washroom, but her thoughts were still on the scene back at the docks. Anger at him and bewilderment at herself vied for her attention. Then she saw herself in the mirror. Except for her eyes and brows that had been covered by the goggles, her face was a featureless mask of white paint. No wonder he had laughed! She was a ridiculous caricature, with the closely tied bandanna and the white face from which her eyes stared, large and seemingly darker than they actually were. With horror she recalled her haughty posturing, which must have added a final clownish touch. Well, she could almost laugh herself. Suddenly remembering Mr. Hawke's imminent appearance, she hastily splashed turpentine on a cloth and scrubbed her face.

Making herself presentable took far longer than she had anticipated, but at last her brown hair hung soft and shining, curling at her shoulder. Her makeup was in place, and she wore the white slacks and the green, crew-neck T-shirt with the white piping that she had brought with her that morning. Looking in the mirror at her face, she noted that her cheekbones looked higher due to the hollows beneath them. She knew she had been losing weight in the last five weeks, for her clothes were loose, but she had taken little notice of herself other than to see that her makeup was even and her hair combed. She had been too busy with other concerns. Now, looking critically at herself, she knew she was already too thin, with the season barely started. What would she look like by December, when it ended?

She was brought up sharply by a sudden thought. The man she met on the dock had prompted this self-inventory. That lazy, shiftless river bum, who had attracted her by nothing more than his looks, had caused

11

her to become aware of herself in a way she had not been for a long time. When, she wondered, had she last had a date other than with Barry Mead, or visited with a friend? She actually did not know. It was not that she lacked interest; there just never seemed to be time. She met many people here at the marina, so many, in fact, that she was never lonely, but still her life had become concentrated on one thing and one thing only: saving the marina for her father. In a sense she had postponed her own life until the problems here were resolved. First she had given up college, then she had given up friendships and dates, until finally her entire life was the marina and her father. Oh, she had had dates with Barry Mead, but he was available and fitted well into her life at the marina, having bought the Side Wheel Restaurant from her father. Barry was interested in her, and she liked him well enough, so she went out with him. It was hardly fair to Barry, now that she thought of it, for recently she had begun to suspect that to him the dates were more than just casual. Other than those dates the only thing she did for relaxation was to scour the river islands for driftwood.

It was no wonder, living the life she did, that the sight of an attractive man – no matter how unprepossessing he was otherwise – had swept her off her feet. She had been struck dumb, and had stood there gawking like a teen-ager at a movie idol. Well, she refused to make a point of avoiding him, but she would treat him with a cool disinterest that even he could not misinterpret. And tonight she would talk to her father, not just talk but even threaten him. Although she knew she could never desert him, she would use every weapon at her command to bring him to his senses.

Kimberly walked into the store, a woman with her mind made up, and there he was lounging against the counter.

"Is it really you?" he asked grinning, his black eyes raking her appreciatively.

"I'm sorry, I'm busy right now," Kimberly told him, picking up a sheaf of papers from behind the counter, and carrying them to the desk in the far corner of the room.

She was unaware that he had followed her and was startled by his voice directly behind her, saying, "I'm busy too, but it doesn't make me rude."

"Rude!" She spun around to face him. "You're a fine one to talk about being rude." He was so close, she tried to back away and bumped the desk chair in her awkward effort. "I've never met anyone as rude as you are, and I don't want to know you."

His black eyes glinted knowingly into her

angry ones. "That's a hard line to take. Why make any hasty decisions? It's possible we could be friends if you would stop glowering at me and forget I caught you looking like something out of the ragbag."

Even as her rage mounted, she wondered why she cared what he said. She would have moved away, but she was backed into a corner, the desk on one side and the chair behind her, bumping the wall. He leaned close, too close, his eyes laughing into hers. Whatever words she had been about to say fled, and she stared mutely back into his compelling black eyes. Her thoughts scattered and her mind groped frantically to regain the anger she knew was there.

But she could only stare back at him, mesmerized for the moment, her amber eyes wide and bewildered as his dark face came closer, until his lips gently touched hers in the lightest of kisses. Still she stood unmoving, like a bird hypnotized by the soft singing of a stalking cat. His arms swept around her, drawing her close, and he bent his face to hers, his lips hard against her mouth. For one mad, delirious moment she lay helplessly pressed against him and then something seemed to explode in her mind and she came alive in his arms, arching away from him, her hands flat against his chest, forcing him away. Her anger

14

returned in a wild surge of fury. She struck at him with one hand and then the other, but he was too quick and imprisoned both her wrists, laughing down into her angry face as she tried to pull away from him.

"You are a little cat, aren't you?" he said. There was no anger in his voice, only amusement.

"Let me go," she gasped.

"Is it safe to let you go?"

Not answering, she dragged her hands from his clutch, feeling a stunned, bewildered rush of fear.

"I told you we could be friends," he was saying. "You'll have to learn not to fight so hard against it." There was hateful laughter in his voice, the glow of victory in his eyes.

"Get out." The words came through Kimberly's clenched teeth. She needed time to think, time to compose herself. How had this happened, her mind shrieked silently. How had she stood there and let it happen?

"Calm your ruffled feathers. A kiss isn't all that important. You act like you've never been kissed before."

"Get out!"

"All right. Another day, another time. But I can't get out immediately. I have to make a phone call. How much do I owe you?"

He was taking his wallet from his hip

15

pocket, opening it and waiting for her answer, all business now, as if the kiss and her own unbelievable response had never occurred. But Kimberly could only look blankly at him, unable to grasp what he meant or why he was paying her.

"How much rental for mooring here for a week?"

She told him through stiff lips, and then listened numbly while he called Alton and ordered a rental car.

"Yes, Cartwright's Landing. This afternoon? Good. Christopher Hawke on the *Pandora.*" As he hung up he smiled at Kimberly, who still stood defensively against the chair. "I'll be seeing you around," he said and chucked her under the chin, at which she started violently, trying to back away as if under attack. Once more he threw his head back and laughed at her. Then, shaking his head, he turned toward the door, still chuckling.

Kimberly sank weakly onto the desk chair, her unseeing eyes on the door where he had disappeared. It was not, as he had implied, his kiss that had shaken her so badly, but her own response to his kiss. What had happened to her that she had allowed this strange man to take her in his arms and kiss her like that? With his eyes looking into hers and his face

16

close above her, all of her self-determination had fled. As if he had imposed his will on her, she had been helpless to do anything but what he dictated. For one insane moment she had even responded to his kiss. "My God, what happened to me?" she asked aloud of no one in particular.

Gradually, as her thoughts slowed and her heart ceased its mad beating, she began to try to explain to herself her almost inexplicable actions. Not given to introspection or self-analysis, she found it was a slow and difficult process. Her mind went back to that moment when she first saw him on the deck of the cruiser and a disquieting flutter went through her at the memory, but she quickly subdued it with the thought of his mocking laughter. It was just physical attraction, she decided, because she actively disliked the man. Then she remembered her idle musings in the washroom before he came into the store. Yes, it was easily explained: her life was arid. She was twenty-two years old and did none of the things she should be doing. Her whole life was work and worry. After she had seen a man whose looks attracted her, her repressed emotions had taken over. It had nothing to do with that man, she assured herself. She was like someone in a desert, desperately thirsty and suddenly seeing water.

17

But despite her logical explanation Kimberly could still see vividly, in her mind's eye, flashing black eyes in a copper-tan face smiling down at her.

CHAPTER 2

Determined to catch her father before he left for the evening, Kimberly went home in the late afternoon, driving up the River Road toward the lowering sun that hung above the scattered islands and the wooded point of land that marked the confluence of the Illinois and Mississippi rivers. At the entrance to Elsah she paused, her eyes drinking in the quiet peace of the little village already in partial shadow from the high bluff on its western side. Shadows were a feature of Elsah, for another bluff, which threw shade until midmorning, towered on the east. Nestled between the two bluffs, the town was two streets wide and only six deep, protected and contained by the sheltering bluffs. It was an old village that had changed little with the years. Kimberly had grown up here but not until she returned from college had she fully appreciated its quaint uniqueness.

Nowhere else was there a town so untouched by modern progress, for the old houses, many of them of native stone, had stood since the middle of the last century, still sheltering the descendants of the original builders. Kimberly's own house was of pale, creamy stone, two stories high, *L*-shaped, with a narrow porch set in the angle of the *L*. Like so many of the houses, it was built close against the sidewalk, land being precious in the narrow valley. Two maples had been planted in the narrow verge of grass between the street and the sidewalk, and they towered high above the second story, throwing the house into perpetual shade. Their trunks, four feet in diameter, had long ago uprooted the sidewalk so that now they stood in the walkway and had to be skirted by pedestrians.

Kimberly found Richard Cartwright in the kitchen, seated at the round maple table with a cup of black coffee before him. He wore a fresh, blue sport shirt and slacks, and the scent of his after-shave mingled with the aroma of coffee. His hair, the same rich brown as her own except for the streaks of silver at the sides, had been carefully combed, but the ravages of the all-night spree were evident in his red-rimmed, dark-circled eyes. Unwilling to greet him with the vituperative

19

words that hovered on her tongue, Kimberly went behind the partition that separated and hid the modern utilities of the kitchen from the primitive, Early American decor of the rest of the room. Pouring a cup of coffee for herself, she came back to the table and sat opposite him.

She could see that he was, as usual, ashamed of himself but too defensive to make excuses. Or perhaps, Kimberly thought, it was just that everything that could be said had been said in previous arguments.

"I had to have a mechanic come to repair the *Quinn's* engine," she told him, the implication clear that he should have been there to repair the engine himself.

He watched her spoon sugar into her coffee, and when her eyes met his again, he said, "I know, Kitten, you've been working too hard. It isn't fair to you, and I've decided to do something about it."

Kimberly sat quietly looking at him, the spoon stilled in her hand. In the past there had always been assurances that everything would be all right, or promises that he was planning to do better.

"I've given it a lot of thought and decided we can't keep the marina."

"Can't keep it? Why, we can't sell it! We can't afford to sell it. What would we do?

20

How would we live?" Nothing had prepared her for this. Not even the sale of the Side Wheel last year had sparked the least idea that they might sell the marina.

"Well." He hesitated. "I've been thinking, Kitten, that if you took a regular job with decent hours, you could do all right. You could even get a job in Saint Louis. A lot of people out here work in Saint Louis. You could have your choice of jobs there."

"And what do you think I could do? I can't make enough to support us." Her eyes narrowed suspiciously as the reason for this sudden decision dawned on her.

"And what would you do?" she asked, her voice laden with suspicion.

"I can always get work as a mechanic."

"You can work as a mechanic in your own marina."

"You know my heart isn't in it any longer. I don't want the responsibility of my own business. It makes demands – I just would feel better if I worked for someone else."

"Then go to work for someone else, but don't talk about selling the marina. Maybe you won't always feel like this."

"I don't think I'll change. I haven't changed in these three years."

It was not a bid for sympathy, Kimberly knew, for Richard Cartwright never asked for pity, but the very tone of it was not like him. If he wanted the money to finance his gambling, as she suspected, he would have merely stood on his rights to sell what was his if he wanted to.

"Wouldn't it be better for you if you didn't have to worry about the marina?" he said, interrupting her musings. "You'd have time to do the things a young girl should do. You could marry Barry Mead, if that's what you want –"

"I don't want to marry Barry Mead, I just want to know what this is all about. I've worked long and hard to keep the marina going and I deserve to know the truth." She leaned forward across the table, her eyes demanding and relentless on his face.

"All right," he finally sighed, as he slumped back in his chair in an attitude of defeat. "I lost heavily last night. I never before played on credit, but I did last night."

Kimberly felt a sinking weakness wash through her. All the long, hard hours to keep the marina operating, all the petty economies of everyday living, all the long-held hopes that Richard would finally come back to himself, the lost schooling, the lost years – all of it for nothing, for defeat like this.

"How much?" she finally asked in a strangled voice.

There was pain in his face and a look that asked for forgiveness.

"Three thousand dollars."

It might as well have been three million. There was no way they could pay it.

"A man called me today," Richard was saying. "A Mr. Hawke. You remember, Dr. Benning asked us to hold that slip for him? Well, he's here now and he called. He wants to buy the marina."

Kimberly heard his words, but her thoughts were on the future. Any work she found could only pay a trifling salary and when the money from the marina was gone, what would her father do? He would just have to work but sometimes she wondered if he was well enough to work. He had a way of suddenly sitting down in the nearest chair and when he stood, he often leaned against walls or furniture as if the effort was too much for him. He had scoffed at her suggestions that he see a doctor, saying he had just missed a meal and it had made him a little weak. She knew he missed many meals and suspected he missed more than she knew, for he was painfully thin. Only the nagging worry about his health had kept her from insisting that he do the mechanic's work at the marina, as he had in the past.

The clatter of the door knocker brought

23

Kimberly to her feet. As she moved through the hall and across the small foyer, she hoped it was not a neighbor who had chosen this moment to stop for a visit, for her mind was like a tethered horse plunging wildly in every direction for a way to be free. To her the loss of the marina would be nothing less than catastrophic. Richard would never change and, when the money from the sale was gone, they would live on the edge of poverty with only the money she could earn to support them.

When she opened the door, her thoughts snapped quickly back into focus at the sight of the black-haired man from Mr. Hawke's boat. Her amber eyes widened in surprise and then narrowed in resentment, but she quickly realized by his questioning look that he was as surprised to see her as she was to find him knocking at her door.

"What do you want?" she asked ungraciously.

The glint was back in his eyes, and the shadow of a grin played about his mouth as he said, "Christopher Hawke," bowing his head in almost formal introduction, "to see Mr. Cartwright."

Kimberly stared in surprise. He was Christopher Hawke? Not a river bum, as she had thought, but Christopher Hawke, the

24

friend of Dr. Benning and the owner of the *Pandora?* Then her original impression of him shifted, and instead of the brash, careless river bum who did as he pleased and boldly took advantage of every opportunity offered, he suddenly became the powerful, inconsiderate man of wealth who took advantage of every opportunity as if it was his god-given right.

"May I come in? Or do I have the wrong house?"

"Come in, Mr. Hawke. You have the right house." It was Richard Cartwright speaking from behind her. Kimberly stepped back, opening the door wider to allow him to enter. "This is my daughter, Kimberly."

"We met this afternoon," he said, flashing a glance at her.

They sat in the parlor, a room furnished much like the kitchen but with a couch and several armchairs as concessions to comfort. The blue Oriental rug was the keynote to the room, and among the browns and tans of the furnishings there were touches of that same soft, deep blue.

Kimberly had little to say but she listened in silent resentment as Richard explained that she had been managing the marina for the past three years and that it was too much for her. Richard did not exactly lie, but he cautiously skirted the truth.

25

"The hours are too long for a girl to work," he explained. "She should have time for a social life. You know, dates, girl friends.

"It's a good marina. I haven't lost money on it even one season. And I don't know if you're aware of it, but there aren't many other yards on this side of the lake. On the other side, yes, but the people who use this side don't have to put up with all the traffic there is on the other side."

"What about that side-wheeler?" Hawke asked. "Would that be available?"

"Well, no. We sold that last year. With Kimberly doing most of the work, it took a lot off her shoulders by letting it go."

Hawke's eyes turned to Kimberly, quietly studying her face. There was no flash of amusement there now, but a penetrating gaze that seemed to read her thoughts, assess her value, and finally categorize her. Then his glance flickered back to Richard, and Kimberly could read in his face that he had not been deceived. He knew, as surely as if he had been told, that Richard was desperate to sell the marina. And why not? Looking at the marina, he could see the evidence of neglect. Then there was the damning sale of the Side Wheel. With burning embarrassment Kimberly suspected that by looking at Richard, he could see the telltale signs of

26

the habitual drinker. The only thing he could not know about was the gambling. Then, with a surge of hope, Kimberly realized that the shabby appearance of the marina might be the saving of it, for there was no reason why a profitable business like that should go downhill just because she was managing it; if she had had the use of the profits, it would look the same now, if not better, than it had three years ago.

Richard was talking again, mentioning figures and numbers, but Hawke interrupted him. "I think the possession of that side-wheeler would be important, though. All my marinas have a clubhouse for the guests. I find the clubhouse itself attracts people. A mooring for a boat can be found anywhere, but a clubhouse creates an attractive atmosphere. Then, too, with the clubhouse it's possible to charge more for the moorings. Of course you haven't many slips for large boats and that's another thing that would have to be changed."

"But there's land for enlargement," Richard told him. "I own all that land where the dry docks and work sheds are, and I built them back far enough to allow for enlarging the harbor without having to move them."

"Well, if you'll give me the name of the owner of the side-wheeler, I'll talk to him

And I want to look at the books too." Then, turning to Kimberly with the attitude of a man who has finished with business for the time being, he said, "I thought you were one of those little river bums. You did look like one."

"And I thought the same about you. You acted like one," she snapped at him. This man was her enemy. His very presence threatened her father's future. Perhaps Richard was too blind, too stubborn, or too lacking in interest to see it, but she knew and refused even to pretend to a semblance of politeness. "Tell me," she said, watching him through narrowed eyes, "did you come here for the express purpose of buying our marina?"

"I came to look at it. Doctor Benning seemed to think you might be willing to sell, and he knows I'm always interested in any marinas that come on the market."

"And why did Doctor Benning assume we would be willing to sell?"

Hawke shrugged noncommittally. "I'm sure you know more about that than I do."

"You made that long trip down the Illinois River just to look at Cartwright's Landing?" There was both doubt and accusation in her voice, for a suspicion that Richard was in some way involved in his arrival was growing in her mind.

28

"I came to buy it if I liked what I saw. And I always travel by water if I have the time and can possibly do it. There's no need for you to look so suspicious. Everything is aboveboard. Your marina isn't the first one I've gone a long way to see."

"Well, you can leave because you're wasting your time here. We aren't going to sell."

She felt more than saw Richard's surprised look, for her eyes were still on Hawke, who seemed unimpressed by her rudeness.

"Kimberly doesn't want to sell the marina," Richard said by way of apology. Then turning to Kimberly, he said, "Kitten, Mr. Hawke called this morning, and I invited him here."

Kimberly was looking stormily at her father, unwilling to argue with him in the presence of this man Hawke, when the door knocker sounded again.

She leaped to her feet, eager to be away from both of them. When she opened the door and saw Barry Mead on the porch, she recalled that she had made a dinner date with him. At first she was glad to see him, happy for the interruption, but then she realized that she would have to go upstairs and change, leaving him with Hawke and her father. If she did that, there would be the opportunity for Hawke to offer to buy the Side Wheel Restaurant, and until

29

could talk to Barry, she hoped to avoid that confrontation.

"Can we just go somewhere where I won't have to dress?" she asked, slightly breathless.

"If you want to. But why? You so seldom will take the time off to go out to dinner I thought you would like to go somewhere nice."

"I'll explain," she said, lifting her purse from the foyer table and closing the door behind her as she stepped onto the porch.

Barry had suggested several places, but they ultimately agreed on a tiny little restaurant in Alton that had good food and the added asset of very private, high-backed booths. During the drive Kimberly was silent, so silent that Barry, not always discerning, was prompted to ask what was wrong.

"I'll tell you when we get there," Kimberly said and fell again into gloomy contemplation.

"Now tell," Barry said when they were in one of the booths and had given their order to a bored waiter.

She explained the situation, omitting her own earlier meeting with Christopher Hawke and concentrating on the basic facts.

"He wants to meet you and ask you to sell e Side Wheel to him too," she finished.

"Well, that, at least, is good news."

"Good news!"

"It hasn't worked out, Kimberly. Having to close the place from the beginning of December to the beginning of April is a dead loss on my investment. Then, too, I can't keep regular help. Having to hire new people every spring means that someone has to break them in. You know the food isn't as good as it is at my restaurant here in Alton. A good cook won't stay in a seasonal job."

Barry was tall and thin with an angular jaw, a long nose, and large blue eyes with sweeping lashes that Kimberly often remarked were a waste on a man. Now his eyes were wide and questioning, as if asking why she could not see that this was so.

"Then you'd sell to him if he offered to buy?"

"No, not if you asked me not to."

"But it would be foolish for you to keep it?" He only gazed silently at her and she sighed. "I'm sorry, Barry. It's unfair of me to put you in this position. Of course you have to sell if it was a poor investment in the first place."

"That isn't what I was thinking; I'm wondering why you're so vehement about it. You sound like you hate this man Hawke, yet you really can't blame him because your father wants to sell the marina."

31

"If he weren't there offering to buy it, Dad couldn't sell."

"Oh, but I think he would."

"What do you mean?"

"You do Dick an injustice, Kimberly. We were talking last week, and he said he was worried about you. He said you work too many hours at the marina, and if he sold it, you could have a more normal life."

"But that's ridiculous! I can't support both of us with the kind of job I might be able to get."

"He doesn't expect you to support him. He would work too. He just doesn't want the responsibility of owning the marina. You have to admit you would be better off."

"Oh, yes, I'd be better off. But he just doesn't think of the future. What if he doesn't work? He didn't even repair Quinn's motor last week."

"I think he would go to work. The point I'm trying to make is he is not selling the marina just for the money, as you seem to think. He wants an easier life for you."

Kimberly gazed mournfully back at Barry. "I can't let him do it," she finally said. "He's not old. He might change. As long as he has the marina he'll have a reason for changing."

"Kimberly, marry me."

She felt surprised and then annoyed that he had picked a time like this to talk about marriage.

"Marry me, and all your problems will be solved. You won't have to worry about your father; he can live with us."

At the tone of his soft voice Kimberly's annoyance vanished in shame. Barry was so good, so considerate, and she was certain he had not purposely chosen a moment like this to propose. In the face of her obvious desperation he had thought to ease her problems by offering this solution now. She smiled fondly at him, thinking that she hated to hurt him by an outright refusal, but it was a fitting end to this miserable day that she would have to tell him no.

"It's a poor reason for marrying," she told him, hoping to avoid a more direct answer.

"I had hoped it would not be the only reason." He sounded so prim and proper when he talked like that, Kimberly thought.

"Barry, I can't think of marriage now. I can't think reasonably about anything."

"All right, I won't press you. But keep it in mind; think about it. Will you do that?"

"Barry, I don't –"

"Just think about it." He interrupted her looking stubborn. "I don't want an answ now."

"All right, Barry," she said meekly, but she was certain that he knew she had been about to say she did not love him.

CHAPTER 3

Kimberly arrived at the marina later than usual the next morning. She had lingered over breakfast talking to Richard, who was still adamant in his decision to sell to Hawke if he could. Although Richard had admitted nothing, Kimberly left the house convinced that Barry was right and that it was only for her sake that her father was willing to part with the business that had been such a pride to him in years past, and could be his only lifeline in the future.

A depression tinged with frustration hung over Kimberly as she stood in the parking lot, gazing out across the marina to the river beyond, where the water sparked a delicate fluorescent blue. It was one of those delicious spring days when the sky, the water, and the air seemed calculated to please and charm. Such rare, delicate days should be cherished, and the idea of attending to the small, prosaic tters that normally filled Kimberly's days was repellent to her. With sudden decision and a feeling of casting off cares, she decided that she deserved a holiday, and what better way to spend it than among the myriad islands of the lake, looking for driftwood. She had not been out on the lake since last fall, and the fact that all the wood she had collected then had already been sold gave her an excuse.

She used an old rowboat with an outboard motor that served her purpose well, for with its flat bottom she could run it aground on the islands, wade the short distance to shore, and start her search. The wind was soft in her face, the sun bright on her hair as she skimmed across the river. Hoping to improve the pale golden tan that was all she ever seemed to attain, she wore shorts, a halter top, and old canvas shoes. She often had to wade in the shallow waters around the islands to retrieve half-submerged wood.

The island she had chosen was a small one, almost round, with a strange ring of sand beach circling it that rose slightly higher than the edges of the island. In the declivity between the ridge of sand and the island's true beach, shallow water formed a moatlike defense that also circled the island. What Kimberly found most fascinating was the pristine wilderness of these islands, which seemed to have never known the presence of man.

She grounded her boat on the ridge of sand, waded the few feet to shore, and sloshed through the water lilies that dappled the surface of the moat with their padlike leaves. There was something mesmeric in the search for driftwood that was like a combination of treasure hunt and adventure, a feeling enhanced by the sense of peace that always descended on her when she was alone on one of these deserted islands.

Her eyes alert for any promising piece of wood, Kimberly wandered along the perimeter of the island, walking through weeds and sand and often wading in the moat. She had already made two trips to the boat, her carrying bag – a piece of canvas stretched between two rods – full each time. Occasionally she glanced out across the lake where the white triangles of sailboats dotted the blue water, but they were far-off and did not intrude on her privacy or disrupt the utter tranquillity.

There had been no sound but the soft breeze ruffling the trees and the murmur of the water, and when his voice came from a short distance behind her, she started violently, her heart seeming to leap and then plunge.

"May I ask why you're collecting firewood at this time of year?" As she spun around and Hawke saw her pale face and defensive stance, he said, "I'm sorry. I didn't mean to startle you."

"Well, you did. Why are you always sneaking up on people?"

"It hardly seemed possible that you didn't hear me after the encounter I had with those weeds back there."

In proof of what he said, Kimberly saw the green burrs clinging to his white slacks that were wet to the knees.

"What are you doing here?" she asked, slightly resentful at his intrusion.

"I saw you leave, and when you didn't come back, I followed you. It wasn't hard to spot your boat."

"Why?"

"Because it was in plain view on the beach."

"I mean why did you follow me?" She thought vaguely that he had come to talk her into selling the marina, but, looking at him, she felt a skittering disquietude along her nerve endings. The memory of his arms around her the day before was in the forefront of her thoughts. Instead of the resentment she should feel at the recollection, there was only a vulnerable helplessness.

"To lure you into a feminine weakness so I

37

can take advantage of you with another kiss?" There was laughter and mockery in his face and voice, as if he had read her mind.

Although her anger flared and she could feel heat rising in her face, she said nothing, refusing to give him the satisfaction of a display of temper.

When she finally spoke, her voice was cool, controlled. "I thought you might have come with the intention of trying to persuade me to sell the marina. I won't sell. Never."

"Why should I do that? It's your father's marina; if he wants to sell it, he will. And if I want to buy it, I will. And if he doesn't want to sell though I want to buy, I'll find a way to – encourage him. You see, I always get what I want."

His arrogance was insufferable. Kimberly had never before met anyone whose confidence was so invulnerable that he found no necessity for making concessions to appearances, even refusing to give lip service to the niceties.

"You're rude," she said, thinking that that was too pale a word to describe him. "You don't even know what common courtesy is. You're like a savage." Her anger at him was tinged with amazement, for it occurred to her that such an attitude must be a beautifully free way to live: know what you want and take it, without any stabs of conscience to bother you. Of course, that was provided you had the money to do it. But somehow she felt a lack of money could never stop Christopher Hawke.

"Perhaps you're right; I might be like a savage, but it's a simple way to live. Why clutter up your life by saying a lot of things you don't mean? It's a waste of time and only serves to confuse people and shadow your true thoughts.

"Come on. I'll help you collect firewood." Without waiting for her to agree, he began scooping up every piece of wood nearby.

Kimberly stared at him uncertainly, then began to laugh. "No. No, I'm collecting driftwood."

"Well, here's some, but you should have something larger than that little piece of canvas to carry it in."

"I don't want that." She was still laughing as he tossed several more small tree trunks on the growing stack of wood he had swiftly collected. "I only want decorative driftwood."

He straightened, looking at her ruefully and scratching his head. "You seem to have hit on one of my areas of utter ignorance. What is decorative driftwood?"

"Why, it's wood that has been in the water a long time. It's smoothed and warped by the river, not all sodden like some of that. It's hard and gray."

"And people decorate with it?"

"Yes. The smaller pieces are used indoors. The larger ones can be used in landscaping."

He stood staring at her for a moment and then asked, "You sell it?"

There was a probing incisiveness to his voice and the few moments of friendliness between them were gone. To Kimberly his tone implied the discovery of a new depth of desperation in her obvious poverty.

"Yes, I sell it," she told him acidly. "You can use just so much driftwood, and since I collect it for a hobby, I can't just keep it stored. I've been doing it since I was first allowed to go out alone in a boat. If you've only come here to pry, then you can just leave; you can probably use it as another reason to convince my father that he should sell the marina. And since you always get what you want, I can only assume you mean you pay more than a thing is worth, and I'll be sure to tell him that. If you do manage to buy Cartwright's Landing, I'll see to it that you pay dearly."

He heard her out, untouched by her anger.

"You misunderstood," he told her calmly when she had finished. "I was curious because it's a business I had never heard of. It might

40

be worth investigating. I never pass up an opportunity. If there's a market for driftwood, it wouldn't take much of an investment to hire boys to collect it."

"I hardly think it would be worth your time," Kimberly said, feeling slightly foolish and very subdued.

"Maybe not, but show me what it is we're looking for, and let's collect some of the valuable stuff."

To Kimberly's surprise she found he could be very pleasant company. They laughed a lot, especially when he retrieved ugly misshapen blobs of wood and brought them to her for inspection. Once he waded out into the lake and suddenly floundered onto a step-off and almost disappeared under the surface.

"I shouldn't laugh," Kimberly told him, tears of amusement in her eyes as she sat on the beach after he came out, wet, bedraggled, trailing a leafed vine over his shoulder. "It is, after all, a river and those step-offs can be dangerous."

"They can," he said seriously. "Did you ever go off one?"

"No. I'm more careful. If I can't see the bottom, I feel my way along. I wouldn't go that far unless I could see that the wood was resting on the bottom. That one you went after was bobbing along in the current."

41

On the downriver end of the island the beach was broad and here, after sharing the lunch Kimberly had brought, they stretched out in the mild sun. The afternoon was far gone, both their boats piled with driftwood, and they were peacefully enjoying well-earned relaxation when Kimberly recalled something from the conversation of the night before.

"You said last night that most of your marinas have clubhouses. Do you own a lot of marinas?"

"Sixteen."

His voice was sleepy, and he had thrown his arm across his face to protect his eyes from the sun so he failed to see the surprise on Kimberly's face. Sixteen marinas! she was thinking. He must be fabulously wealthy. And he certainly talked like a man of wealth. Slowly an idea was forming in her mind, a scheming idea that was foreign to her usual upright nature. If he was that wealthy and still had money to invest, she might be able to convince him that owning half of a marina would be as good as the whole. She would insist on banking the money in her own name so that she could pay their half of the expenses, but even more to the point was the fact that someone else would be paying the other half. She knew that with such an arrangement, she could hire back all the men she had had to let go. She could spend only a reasonable amount of each day there and still manage the marina. And eventually, when Richard was ready, he would have his business and the life that had meant so much to him in the past. But she would wait until she knew Hawke better and not rush into anything too precipitously.

In the meantime she would be very nice to him. Yesterday the idea of being nice to him would have seemed impossible, even useless, but this had been an enchanted day, and Christopher Hawke no longer seemed the monster he had the night before. Even his self-confidence held a masculine charm now that he was no longer using it against her.

Kimberly cast a cautious glance at him, noting the clear copper-tan skin and the thick black hair glinting blue in the sun as it dried.

"By the way," he said, startling her, for she thought he was asleep. "Do you have a maid at the marina?"

"A maid?"

"Yes. I need someone to clean the *Pandora*." Lifting his arm from his face, he turned to look at her. "You don't have a maid. Well, do you know anyone around here who does housecleaning?"

"Yes – yes, I think Mrs. Kramer would be glad to have some work like that. I'll ask her."

Kimberly looked at his black eyes under the winging black brows and thought with a tiny thrill that she could find it very easy to be nice to him. But a warning tolled in her memory, telling her that today she had seen the softer, more cheerful side of Christopher Hawke, a side that was not perhaps as indicative of his nature as the hard glint in his eyes when he had said, "I always get what I want."

CHAPTER 4

As Hawke helped Kimberly unload the two boats and carry the driftwood to a storage building near the paint shed, he had suggested they go to the lodge of Père Marquette State Park for dinner the following evening.

"We'll take the *Pandora*," he said. "Do you like traveling on the river?"

"I love it," Kimberly had confessed, not mentioning that she seldom had the opportunity to travel in such grand style.

Now, as she stood before her mirror surveying the results of two hours of primping, she recalled how often during the long day her thoughts had been on Hawke. Early that morning he had walked up to the parking lot, a duffel bag slung over his shoulder, waved casually to her as he passed and, tossing the bag carelessly into the backseat of the rented car, had driven off toward Alton. It was probably his laundry, she surmised, thinking he would soon return. But the day had dragged at a snail's pace, and if he had returned before her early departure, she had missed seeing him.

She would do, she decided, touching her bright brown hair where it curled at her shoulder. Her dress was new, the only new outfit she owned, and it was one of the latest soft styles, the full gathered skirt airy and billowing, the bodice clinging but not tight beneath the open, scooped neck, and the wide sleeves falling in a dip at her elbows. But it was the luscious color that had attracted her, a golden apricot that darkened her amber eyes and looked like a confection.

At the marina she wore nothing on her face but a touch of lipstick, but tonight she had applied a full complement of makeup, including eye shadow and mascara. She had to admit it did much for her and she thought, too, that it emphasized a maturity that was not evident without it.

The door knocker sounded below, and almost immediately she heard Richard's steps in the hallway. Their voices mingled in greeting as she came to the head of the stairs; then, as she started down, Hawke, having heard her sandals on the steps, looked up.

For a moment he merely stared, then a hot light leaped in his dark eyes, and they fastened on her, seeming to inventory every movement but finally coming to rest on her face. Kimberly felt seared by that burning gaze, and even as she felt the heat rising above the neckline of her dress and flooding into her face, she wondered how black eyes, which she always considered cold, could seem to burn like this.

She was too flustered to notice the exchange between Hawke and Richard as they left. Then, when they were in the car and he turned to stare at her, she felt outraged anger at herself replacing the confusion. Why, she wondered, was she being so foolishly adolescent? Men had looked at her before with appreciation; before her life had become so busy, she had seldom been without a date.

"You're a veritable Cinderella," Hawke told her.

Kimberly raised her brows and her lips curved in a tiny smile. "I don't know whether to thank you for the compliment or stop speaking to you for the insult."

"You can't stop speaking to me. Haven't you realized yet that I'm Prince Charming?"

46

"A fine Prince Charming you are, falling in the river and standing there gawking in the foyer." She hoped that by accusing him of gawking she could learn whether or not he had noticed her own confusion under his assessing stare.

"I had reason to gawk, as you call it. I didn't know I was dealing with a grown woman. You've been masquerading as a little girl."

Kimberly smiled complacently. "It's your own fault if you can't distinguish a grown woman from a little girl."

"Well, how old are you?"

"Don't you know that is a question you should never ask?"

"Not with you. You're neither old enough nor young enough to have to lie."

He had started the car as he spoke, and while his attention was on the narrow streets of Elsah, Kimberly studied his profile, trying to place his age; he was at least thirty, she finally decided. For the first time it dawned on her that for all she knew, he might be married. The thought was startling, unwelcome, and brought with it an imperative need to know.

"Well?" he asked, cocking an eyebrow toward her.

"Well, what?"

47

"How old are you?"

"Twenty-three. And since we're asking personal questions, it occurs to me that I know nothing about you. You could be married with twenty children."

He laughed. "Or I could be childless with five wives."

"Are you?"

"My, you *are* inquisitive. But since it seems important to you, I'm not. I've managed to avoid all that." They were on River Road now, and he turned to look at her, a sardonic grin on his face. "Satisfied?"

"Not entirely," Kimberly snapped. "I asked because I don't go out with married men."

"Then you're more proper than most girls I've met."

"Perhaps it's your taste in girls that's at fault," she told him primly, wondering why they were arguing.

"Then this is your opportunity to educate me in the proper choice of girls."

"I'm not interested in educating you. You can be ignorant for the rest of your life, for all I care."

They had reached the marina, and she sat stubbornly in the car, staring directly ahead as he came around to open the door for her.

"Why do you want to argue?" he asked as

she brushed his hand away and stepped from the car.

"Why do I want to argue? You sneer, you're sarcastic, you're rude, and then you ask me why I want to argue!" It was on the tip of her tongue to say she would not go with him, she preferred to go home, but she looked up into his laughing face and saw such friendly amusement that she was reminded of the day before when they had laughed together on the island. She gave him a small, tentative smile.

"That's better. I won't tease you anymore if it upsets you so."

Despite his words, Kimberly knew he had not been teasing; nevertheless she allowed herself to be led to the *Pandora*.

On the gravel drive near the yacht a man who appeared to be merely loitering became suddenly alert at the sight of them and then hurried to meet them. Kimberly watched him curiously, for he was certainly not here for boating, dressed as he was in a suit, with a tie and white shirt and an attaché case in his hand.

"Mr. Hawke," he said with obvious relief. "I was afraid I wouldn't find you."

"You brought the plans?" Hawke asked.

"Yes." Glancing at Kimberly, he adde "But it can wait until tomorrow. I came soon as they were ready because I knew you were anxious to get this started."

"We're in no hurry. Come aboard and I'll look at them now. Then you can fly back either tonight or tomorrow, whichever is most convenient for you."

As they moved toward the *Pandora*, Hawke introduced him as Bob Davies and explained that he had come down from Chicago with plans for a new marina.

"It's going to be the elite of all the marinas on the lake," Hawke told Kimberly. "They're already dredging out the harbor. It was just a little bay, not nearly large enough for the size marina I'm planning. With enough men working, they might be able to finish it this summer, but I'm not certain about that because there's going to be a large clubhouse, besides cabins scattered in the woods. Then, of course, the locks; some of those will be entirely enclosed for the winter."

"It will be more than just a marina," Bob Davies joined in with enthusiasm. "Really more like a resort. But you'll have to think of something else to call the clubhouse," he told Hawke. To Kimberly he said, "It's going to be like an old southern mansion, pillars and all."

They had arrived at the *Pandora*, and vies spread the plans on the table in the cabin. Kimberly moved close, as Hawke leaned over the table to examine a scaled diagram. Almost immediately he slapped his palm against the drawing and looked up at Davies with an angry frown.

"Did you look at this before you brought it here?" he asked in a cold voice.

"You mean the joined cabins?"

"Yes, I mean the joined cabins, and only two gas pumps, and the clubhouse built close to the road instead of having a lawn in front of it." There was restrained anger in Hawke's voice, and Davies's easy camaradarie faded as he hastily drew another paper from his case.

"Here are the plans drawn the way you requested them, but Selkirk asked me to show you this other one first. He said it would be far cheaper to build the cabins joined because of the need for water and electricity going to all those scattered cabins and the individual air conditioners too."

"I was never unaware of that," Hawke told him coldly.

"Well, he was thinking of later maintenance too. He said the upkeep on the grounds around the clubhouse would be cheaper if there wasn't so much lawn and shrubbery."

"Let me see the other one."

There was silence while Hawke studied the other plans, and when he finally looked

51

again, the anger was gone from his face.

"Well, at least he knew what I wanted." Frowning again, he said, "Did you know he was wasting time on this other drawing?"

"No, not until he showed them to me this morning."

"The man is a fool."

"I think he was just trying to impress you."

"Then he thinks I'm a fool." There was disgust in his voice. "He's supposed to be the best, but he obviously can't take orders."

"He's probably used to doing business with people who are glad to have his recommendations. As you said, he is the best." Davies's tone was casual and he made no attempt to defend Selkirk.

"You can tell him I don't want any more suggestions about cutting corners or saving money. I want him to concentrate on my orders and not waste any more time; if he has countersuggestions for everything I've planned, we'll never finish this before winter."

Kimberly had listened in silence, her eyes turning from one man to the other as they spoke, acutely aware of the air of command in Hawke's attitude. His unconscious authority obviously impressed this man Davies as it did Kimberly herself, and she was aware that what had considered brashness and conceit were, in truth, a self-assurance that was an integral part of Hawke's personality. Despite Hawke's anger and disapproval Davies had not been offended, but had accepted it as Hawke's prerogative. Yet Davies seemed neither meek nor unsure of himself, so his easy acceptance of Hawke's authority could only be based on respect gained from personal knowledge.

Kimberly sat on a stool beside Hawke in the pilot-house that was an adjunct to the main cabin and several steps above it, her attention divided between him and the grand panorama of water and sky. The river was still broad here, part of Alton Lake, reaching almost to the horizon on their left, where the flatlands between the Mississippi and Missouri rivers lay. Closer and on their right, the palisades marched along the river, broken occasionally by a stream flowing into the Mississippi. Myriad wooded islands broke the clear flow of the river, giving the view a wild, uncivilized aspect that was nevertheless peaceful. They sailed toward the afternoon sun that sparkled on the breeze-ruffled water, and Kimberly felt the magic quiet that always descended on her when she was far out on the river, away from the busy activities of ma and his creations. She thought it strange t' she should feel like this when traveling in yacht, a product of man, laden with all the conveniences of modern living.

Occasionally she cast a furtive look at Hawke, who had been quiet except on the rare occasions when he asked the name of an island or remarked about a passing landmark. He was a strange man, she thought, chameleonlike in his sudden changes of personality. One moment he was quiet and companionable, as now, and the next, arrogant and baiting; yet he could also be laughing and gay, as when he had helped her collect driftwood the day before. She could not understand him, and yet he aroused unexpected emotions in her that varied as much as did his own personality. She had decided in a moment of pique that he was not handsome, but now, looking at him cautiously, she knew that the features she had thought too blunt were ruggedly masculine and detracted in no way from his good looks. If this evening went well and there were no more arguments, she thought, she might find the opportunity to suggest that he buy a half interest in the marina.

They turned into the smaller Illinois River where it entered the Mississippi.

"You're very quiet," Hawke said.

"I'm enjoying the river."

You love this life on the river, don't you?"

54

"Yes, I do. I complain because I work too hard at the marina, but I could never really be happy anywhere else. What about you? You seem to live your life on the water."

"I'll have to confess that I knew long ago it was the only life for me. But I knew, too, that I had no intention of being poor."

"So you worked hard and somehow managed to buy all those marinas."

"Something like that."

Kimberly wondered if his reluctance to talk about himself indicated a secretive nature or merely a disinterest in discussing the past. This might be the time to suggest that he buy half of Cartwright's Landing, but somehow the moment did not seem right, and being too precipitate would almost assure failure. She recalled her anger when he had baited her in the car and groaned inwardly at the thought that, only the afternoon before, she had decided she would be very nice to him.

From the dock they could see the Père Marquette Lodge, its limestone-and-log walls partially visible through the trees. It was a huge, rambling building, so at one with its surroundings that it appeared to have grown there as part of the natural landscape, the shake shingles on the many-gabled roof adding to the rustic atmosphere.

"I've never been here before," Hawke s

as they entered the immense hall, walking on the flagstone floors to the edge of the flight of shallow steps that led down to the main lobby. The ceiling vaulted into the high roof, which was supported and braced by log timbers, and one end of the room was dominated by a fireplace fully twelve feet wide, its broad rock chimney disappearing into the roof high above. Rustic tables and chairs were scattered about the room, and Indian rugs decorated both floor and walls. To their right was the stairway rising to the rented rooms above.

When they were seated in the dining room that opened off the lobby, Hawke looked across the table at Kimberly, seeming to study her face. "Tell me something, Kimberly," he finally said. "Why are you so determined to keep the marina? Oh, I know, you love the river, but your home is only a few short blocks from the water and you wouldn't be separated from it if you no longer had the marina."

"It's not for myself that I want to keep it; it's for my father. He hasn't been himself since my mother died, but he won't always be like this. When he's ready, I want the marina to be there for him. You just don't understand how much of his life went into it."

"But you would be better off without it."

Barry had said the same thing. Why did

these men seem to think they knew more about her than she did herself?

"I don't know. I might have to take a job in an office someplace and just loathe it."

She was tempted to probe, to try to discover if he would really buy the marina from Richard, but again she restrained herself, turning the conversation to trivial matters. As she talked she became aware that Hawke was very silent. Through the entire meal he seemed to be watching her, judging, examining, his dark eyes hardly leaving her face.

"Why are you so silent?" she finally asked.

"I'm thinking how lovely you are."

Lovely? She had never thought of herself as lovely. Pretty, perhaps. Or at least pretty when she was not so thin and hollow-cheeked as she was now. But no one had ever before called her lovely.

"I think you're being flattering."

"No, I'm never flattering. Yours is not the classic beauty, but there is something –. It's elusive but it's there. You're not going to try to tell me you're not popular with men?"

"No, I'm not, because it wouldn't be true," she said, laughing slightly at her own frankness.

The sun was low, but twilight was no

yet upon them when they returned to the *Pandora*. There was a charm to the spring evening that made Kimberly sigh with contentment as they entered the cabin. It was a long time, she realized, since she had felt so carefree, so utterly happy. Hawke had opened a cabinet and was lifting down glasses and bottles.

"What will you have?" he asked.

"Whiskey and soda, I guess," she answered, turning to look out the side port, where the western sky was turning to a glory of red and rose behind a scattering of small purple clouds.

"Which in this part of the country means bourbon and sweet soda."

She heard ice tinkling in the glasses, and then he was behind her. As she turned she looked up into his face. Her amber eyes wide, her lips softly parted, she stared, transfixed, into the black eyes so close above her own. His dark face was quiet, almost impassive, and then his arm went around her waist, and she sighed softly as she swayed toward him. Vaguely she was aware of his putting the glass down somewhere behind her before he gathered her into his arms, and then there was only the swirling ecstasy of her arms clinging to him and his lips against hers. It lasted only moments and then, as if a shutter had clicked and bathed the scene in light, she seemed to see herself clinging helplessly to him, lost in an emotion she had never known before. Stunned, bewildered, she leaned back in his circling arms and stared at him, and as she looked a slow smile, a smile of victory, grew on his face.

"Let me go."

"Why?"

"Because . . . Just let me go." Her hands pushed against him as embarrassment swamped her, but her reeling mind kept repeating: *why, why, why had she acted like this?* What had possessed her suddenly to throw herself into his arms?

But for the moment she dared not think about it; she had to find some way to dissemble. "I must be an incurable romantic," she said, trying to keep her voice from trembling.

"If that's what you want to call it," he said. She resented the amusement in his voice, knew he was laughing at her, and then bit her tongue to refrain from answering him as she recalled how brutally honest he could be.

The trip back was silent, so silent that by the time they were again on the Mississippi, Kimberly was ardently wishing he would say something, anything to break the strained atmosphere. But Hawke appeared utterly relaxed, gazing at the scenery with interest, seemingly unaware of her beside him.

He had to turn on the running lights before they reached Cartwright's Landing and, when he maneuvered the craft into the slip and shut down the motor, a country silence hung about them in the soft darkness, lighted only by a silvery moon.

As she started down the steps to the cabin Kimberly felt his hand on her elbow steadying her and then, in the shadowed darkness of the cabin, his hands on her shoulders turned her toward him.

"Kimberly, you're younger than you think," he murmured in a soft voice.

"I don't want to –"

"Don't talk." His hands moved down her arms and then beneath the wide sleeves of her dress, stroking her arms in a slow, sensuous movement.

A fear composed of what had happened at the harbor near Père Marquette Park, and her own inability to judge either him or herself held her rigid.

"And you're lucky that I'm an honorable man."

She would have answered that, but he turned her quickly toward the door and down the ladder to the dock.

60

In the car she turned to him, determined to break her own silence and try to convince him he had judged her wrongly. "Hawke, you were wrong. Nothing had anything to do with you being honorable or dishonorable; I – I've been too intent on work for too long. It was just the day and the trip; it made me – Oh, you probably can't understand anything like that."

"Oh, I can understand, only I don't believe in using fancy words for it."

"You are crude and impossible." They had reached her house, and she leaped out of the car, slamming the door behind her.

"And you are only a romantic." His disbelieving laughter followed her as she fled across the porch.

CHAPTER 5

Kimberly slammed the front door and leaned back against it, a tumult of anger and confusion causing her breath to come in short, sharp gasps. She could hear the engine of his car die away in the early darkness and, picturing in her mind the hateful smile still on his face, she felt a resurgence of the dislike

61

she had felt for him at their first meeting. What right had he to accuse her of things that never entered her mind? He was low, common, and crude; and why, oh, why had she let herself be deceived by his glib tongue and smooth manner?

But even as her mind ranted against him a core of honesty deep within her told her that no matter how hateful he was, it was she herself who had instigated that scene in the cabin of the *Pandora*. There was no way she could explain it even to herself, except that the entire evening had held a strange magic.

Suddenly annoyed with her unproductive thinking, Kimberly hurried up the stairs to change her clothes. Richard was obviously not home, and for once she was grateful to find him gone, for he would certainly have noted her condition.

It was barely dark, the evening stretching empty before her, and Kimberly felt a driving need to dissipate the nervous energy that consumed her. She paced the floor of her room fruitlessly, but this failed to produce the calmness she sought. Her mind kept turning back to the events of the evening, even to recalling the melting surrender she had known as his arms closed around her.

She would clean the house, she suddenly

decided. She would scrub and work until she was exhausted and then go to bed and, she hoped, be able to sleep.

The work did have a soporific effect on her. Much of the furniture, like the house, was very old, for her mother had retrieved many pieces from the attic and the barn loft, refinished them, and brought them again into use. Her ancestors must have been cautiously conservative about discarding outdated possessions, for everything from old butter-churns to tables, chairs, and wardrobes had been gathering dust for years when her mother rescued them. Some of the rooms were perfect examples of primitive Early American, and before her mother's death their home had been one of the most interesting on the tour of old houses that was held each year in Elsah.

Kimberly was on her hands and knees just beginning to clean the plank floor of the kitchen when the door knocker sounded. For a moment she froze, the presence of Hawke still so much with her that she thought he had returned. It was a vast relief to open the door and find Mrs. Kramer on the porch.

"I just wanted to thank you, Kimberly, for recommending me for the work. I cleaned Mr. Hawke's boat today."

"Come in," Kimberly invited, opening the door wider. "Would you like a cup of coffee?"

"Well, I'll come in for a minute; I want to talk to you about something."

Kimberly led the way to the kitchen and behind her Mrs. Kramer's voice went on. "That Mr. Hawke is such a lovely man, and so handsome too. Kimberly, if I were your age, I'd look more than once at him. You know, I think he must have money too. Why, do you know those glasses he has in that liquor cabinet are Waterford; everything on the boat is expensive. And those chairs in the living room – they're real leather."

"Well, I guess most people who own yachts have money. They're expensive toys."

"Did you get to know him very well?" Her bright eyes were shining.

"I met him," Kimberly said, unwilling to add to Mrs. Kramer's store of material for gossip.

As Kimberly disappeared around the partition in the corner Mrs. Kramer settled herself comfortably at the table. "I see you're cleaning. I won't stay long," she said, but Kimberly knew from experience that Mrs. Kramer would not leave until she had learned everything she had come to learn, or, in the face of too many evasions, finally conceded defeat.

"What was it you wanted to talk to me about?" Kimberly asked, hoping to distract

64

her from what seemed to be an avid interest in Hawke.

"Oh, I was thinking. After cleaning Mr. Hawke's boat – I was thinking, Kimberly, you know I can use every little bit of money I can get. There isn't anyone here in town, except Mrs. Coster, who wants work done. I was thinking that if you put a little sign up in the store there at the marina, maybe other people would hire me to clean their boats."

"I'll put up the sign, but most of the boats are small. Dr. Benning's is the only other yacht we have."

"Yes, but, you see, I could go to the other marinas and if they would put up signs too, I might be able to earn quite a little sum."

Returning to the table while she waited for the coffee to perk, Kimberly smiled at the energetic Mrs. Kramer, who was short, slightly plump, and certainly in her late sixties. Living next door to Mrs. Kramer, Kimberly had known and liked her all her life; except for her avid penchant for gossip, she was a kindly, good-natured woman. Mrs. Kramer's gossip was never intended to be catty, but her judgment was poor, and she had an innocent way of repeating conversations verbatim that sometimes had an embarrassing and occasionally a shattering effect on the

65

person quoted. For this reason no one in town would tell her anything unless they were willing to have it repeated. As a result Mrs. Kramer was often frustrated when her questions were turned aside by someone changing the subject.

"You said you met Mr. Hawke?" she said now, her bright eyes alive with interest. "But, Kimberly, wasn't that Mr. Hawke you went out with tonight?"

"Were you peeking?" Kimberly asked in a teasing voice.

"Certainly not. I just happened to be near my front window when his car drove up." Her innocent tone verged on the indignant, so Kimberly refrained from pointing out to her that if she only saw him drive up, how could she know they had gone out together?

"He talked about you when I was on his boat today. Kimberly, I think maybe he likes you. He asked me questions." She waited, hoping Kimberly would evince interest in the questions, but Kimberly stayed stubbornly mute.

With a sigh at the lack of response, she continued. "He wanted to know about you. I told him what a nice girl you are, and I told him about Barry Meade. But I didn't let on that you might marry him."

"What makes you think I'm going to marry

Barry?" Kimberly asked, as she brought the coffee to the table and poured it.

"Well, you don't go out with anyone else anymore. A girl as popular as you were doesn't just stop going with everyone else unless she's really serious."

"Mrs. Kramer, it just happened that way because I've been too busy for dates. I'm not going to marry anyone."

"Oh." Kimberly could tell by the disappointment in Mrs. Kramer's voice that she must have already spread the news of her imminent marriage to Barry all over the town.

"Well, anyway, I told Mr. Hawke about you, and he was very interested. And, Kimberly, I do think he's handsomer than Barry, don't you?"

"I don't know." Kimberly evaded the question.

"Well, don't you even like him a little bit? It shouldn't be hard to like him."

"I hardly know him."

"Oh, I don't know!" She threw up her hands in discouragement. "Girls just aren't the way they used to be. We always enjoyed talking about handsome men."

The clock on the kitchen mantel was chiming twelve when Kimberly straightened up, massaged her aching back, and surveyed

67

the soft wax glow of the random plank floor. For the first time since winter the stone fireplace had been cleaned of ashes, and the entire room seemed to glow with a brightness it had not known for a long time. It was a lovely room, Kimberly thought, her gaze wandering from the sideboard laden with blue china, to the deacon's bench, the Lincoln rocker, and the side tables that held old lamps, their electric converters well hidden. In the center, on the braided rug, was the round dining table surrounded by Windsor chairs, each slightly different from the other. When her mother was alive, the brass, copper, and pewter utensils on the long wall shelf had always gleamed from frequent polishing; now Kimberly noted sadly how tarnished and dull they looked. But it was still a living kitchen, the heart of the house, as it probably had been back in the 1850s when the house was new.

The upsetting memories of the early evening had been forcefully pushed far back in Kimberly's mind as she concentrated on the cleaning, and admired the familiar objects that she was usually too busy to even notice. Now she decided she would take a hot bath and go to bed, for surely sleep would come if she could soak the ache from her back.

She was no sooner in bed, her head snuggled into the pillow and the light blanket pulled about her shoulders, than the memory of Christopher Hawke was back. But she was sleepy, and somewhere in the busy activity of the evening her anger at him had waned. With the memory of his arms about her, his lips against hers, she fell asleep.

By morning Kimberly felt that her perspective had returned. There was nothing about a kiss to upset her. Only the magic of the spring evening had prompted her to encourage his attentions. As she had told Hawke the night before, she was a romantic. If he chose to put his own gross interpretation on her actions, she would refuse to confirm his ideas by arguing with him about it.

Aware as Kimberly was of the end of the marina where the two yachts were moored, she had no sooner arrived than she noticed movement on the deck of Dr. Benning's boat. Hurrying down the gravel drive and onto the dock, she quickly mounted the steps to the deck, only to stop in surprise at the sight of Laurie Benning, the doctor's daughter, stretched out on a deck lounge wearing a skimpy bikini that seemed barely to cover her ample bust. The sight of Hawke, sitting in the shadow of the deck roof, added confused embarrassment to her surprise.

"I'm sorry," she said, looking at Laurie but flicking a quick glance at Hawke. "I thought

69

someone was trespassing; I didn't know you were here."

"Oh, yes. I'm here, all right." Laurie smiled lazily, her eyes on Hawke.

Something about the picture of easy familiarity they presented brought a flood of resentment to Kimberly. She knew Laurie Benning from times past – not well – but she had often noted with amusement that when Laurie accompanied her father on cruises, there was always a contingent of young men about; some were guests on the yacht, others transients, and Laurie appeared to encourage them all. Kimberly had often wondered if Laurie was as free with her favors as she appeared to be.

Now, at the sight of Hawke, a flood of anger possessed her. She looked at Laurie. The girl's delicate, refined features, with a touch of piquant beauty, were very much at variance with her ripe, swelling figure that, as she lay there almost naked, seemed to shriek sensuality. As she looked at them together, Kimberly's initial anger faded to despair as she realized how much they seemed to belong together. Hawke, too, was sensuous, and both were selfish with an easy disregard for others, a shrugging dismissal of anyone or anything that failed to interest them. They shared an arrogance that overrode all obstacles. Even in

70

appearance they complemented each other. Laurie was as blond as Hawke was dark, her long pale hair a perfect foil for his, as black as a raven's wing.

"Well." Kimberly was about to leave when her responsibility as owner of the marina surfaced above the despondency swamping her. "Oh," she said, turning to Laurie. "Is your father coming? Will he be taking the yacht out?" If he was, they might need a mechanic to check the engine.

"No, I just came for a little vacation by myself," Laurie told her, a note of dismissal in her voice.

As Kimberly walked back toward the marine store she realized that Hawke had done no more than nod to her. She could have been an utter stranger, for all the recognition he gave her. Could it be, she wondered, that he was afraid Laurie would learn he had taken her out the night before? But, no, that was foolish; Hawke was the last man in the world to try to hide his activities. No matter what his faults, deception was not one of them. Even as these thoughts fluttered through her mind she knew they were only random musings meant to hide the hollow feeling that engulfed her, a numbness concentrated just beneath her breastbone.

She sought refuge in the marine store,

71

huddled in the chair at the tiny desk in the corner. For long moments she stared unseeingly at the wall and then with a groan she put her face in her hands.

"I'm falling in love with him," she whispered, not aware that she spoke aloud. *How can I be,* her angry mind ranted. *I don't like him. He's hateful. He's arrogant and selfish.* But none of the arguments helped, for she knew that with blind determination she had refused to see it coming. Last night she had known and in agony she realized that Hawke knew too. He had been right when he laughed at her for claiming to be merely romantic. Only he had not meant love; he had been talking about passion. And there was a difference. He might not know it, but she did, for never under any circumstances could she imagine herself so lost in the magic of a kiss with anyone else.

She wanted to cry, to rant and rave with fury. Finally she sighed, took a deep breath, and straightened her shoulders. She would have to stop this. If she let herself go on this way, Hawke would know for sure that she loved him. Even if she suffered all her days, she would keep this secret to herself, for the thought of his laughter seared her soul.

Behind her Kimberly heard the bell above the door tinkle as someone entered, but for

72

the moments it took her to compose her expression, she stayed rigidly where she was, not daring to turn.

"Kimberly." It was Barry's voice.

Turning, she smiled, a taut smile that seemed to stretch her face into a grimace. "What are you doing out here at this time of day?" she asked, surprised that her voice sounded so natural.

"I heard something that I thought I'd better tell you right away," he said, his brow creased with worry.

"Oh? What is it?"

"Let's go over to the Side Wheel and have a cup of coffee. I could use something to eat too."

The Side Wheel was closed during the week, open only on Saturday and Sunday, when the marina was crowded enough to make the restaurant worthwhile, but Kimberly was often in and out of the boat. She usually ate her lunch there, keeping cold cuts and soda in the refrigerator and using the stove, too, if she wanted something hot. Since the Side Wheel was directly across the harbor at this end of the marina, there was no way to reach it by land other than walking the long distance around the entire perimeter of the marina, so Kimberly suggested taking her boat, that was moored near the marine store.

73

People had been arriving, and there was movement and color on the docks, the orange of life jackets, bright against the colorful sport clothes of the boaters. A woman about to board a motor sailer waved and called to Kimberly. It was Julie Dutton. She and her husband owned a cabin cruiser and a motor sailer, and spent all their spare time at the marina. Her two children and husband were already aboard, but she hurried toward Kimberly.

"I was going to find you when we came back," she said, smiling and nodding at Barry. "Those friends that were with us last weekend want to try going out on their own, and I thought I'd reserve a sailer for them."

"I'll keep the best one for them," Kimberly promised. "What's their name? I don't think I met them."

"No, you didn't. You were with some other people when we came back, and we were at the Side Wheel most of the evening. It's Caswell. I have to hurry off now, but we'll have a visit later."

"Let's do that if you have time," Kimberly told her.

As Kimberly and Barry walked away he said, "I don't know how you get anything done around here when you treat everybody like guests in your own home."

"It isn't easy, but they like the personal touch; it makes them feel that it's more than just a place to moor their boats. And since Richard sold the Side Wheel, it's more important than ever."

"I'm sorry I can't keep it open during the week. I know it would make it better for you."

"Oh, Barry, I appreciate your letting me open it when I have to have a place to take people. If we only had somewhere they could go when they come back from boating." She was about to say she would like to put up some kind of a building but the memory of Richard and his talk of selling the marina kept her from even mentioning plans for the future.

"Now what's so important?" Kimberly asked when they were in the kitchen, and she was spooning coffee into a pot, her back to Barry, who sat at one of the old tables for the use of the employees.

"A friend of mine works at the bank," he said.

"Yes." Kimberly encouraged him to go on, plugged in the coffeepot, and came to the table to give him her full attention.

"Someone has been inquiring about Cartwright's Landing."

"Well, it might be Hawke; I heard him tell

Dad he would like to look at the books."

"I don't know who it is, but he wouldn't have to go to the bank to look at the books. And he wasn't asking about books, anyway; he wanted to know about the mortgage."

"Mortgage? What mortgage?"

"The mortgage on Cartwright's Landing," Barry said, looking even more worried. "I don't like to bring you more trouble when you have enough already, but I thought you should know about this."

"But, Barry, there has to be some mistake. If there was a mortgage, I would know. I take care of all the bills and paperwork."

"I know you do, but the fact remains that someone was inquiring, and there is a mortgage."

"Who is this someone?"

Barry shook his head. "I tried to find out, but this friend of mine didn't even see him. He just knows through someone else that they were examining the mortgage papers. He said if he couldn't learn the name, he would at least try to find out what he looks like."

Kimberly sat in stunned silence. Last year when she had confiscated most of the money from the sale of the Side Wheel, Richard had said very little. She knew the money he kept was gone now, but she wondered if he had

76

gone so far as to mortgage the marina to pay his gambling debts.

"Barry, I have to go home. I'll call Dad; if he's there now, I'll talk to him."

"I'm sorry, Kimberly."

"Well, there's nothing for you to be sorry about. It isn't your fault."

"I mean, I'm sorry you have to have one trouble added to another." After a pause, he added, "Did you think over what we talked about the other night?"

Kimberly, already on her feet, stared at him blankly, then suddenly she remembered his marriage proposal.

"Barry, not now. We'll talk about it later, if you don't mind."

Richard was home, and when Kimberly found him in the kitchen, she wasted no time on preliminaries. "I want to know about the mortgage," she told him.

At his lack of surprise, the quiet bracing of his shoulders, she knew it was true: the marina had been mortgaged.

"For how much?" she asked, sinking into the chair across from him, feeling that her knees might buckle at any moment.

"Seven thousand."

Seven thousand! He already owed three thousand in gambling debts; it was like sinking slowly into quicksand.

"When did you mortgage it?" she finally asked.

"Last year."

She thought for long moments and finally said, "So that's why you never had to use credit to gamble. Why didn't I know? Why wasn't there anything about it from the bank?"

As if the last curtain had been drawn away and he stood exposed in his shame, he told her: he had a post-office box in Alton.

"Kitten, I'm going to stop gambling," he said earnestly. "I've never promised you that before, have I?"

She shook her head mutely.

"And have I ever broken a promise to you?"

"No. But if you drink, you'll gamble."

"Not the way I have been. I kept thinking I could get the money back. I haven't gotten it back, at least not enough. I just always get in deeper. That was the reason I had to sell the Side Wheel. I can still gamble; I can play penny-ante stuff. And if you want me to, I'll even join Alcoholics Anonymous. But, Kitten, I want you to know one thing; I would be in favor of selling the marina even if I weren't in debt. I don't want to own it, and I don't want you tied to the long hours and living the way you do now."

"But the hours wouldn't be long if I had the money to hire enough help."

"I know that, but this happened, and I didn't think where I was going until it was too late. I needed the money. Trying to win it back was a fool thing to do, but after I mortgaged the marina, I couldn't see any other way to get it back."

"All right," Kimberly said wearily, rising and looking down at him. "But I still want to try to keep the marina. Maybe there's some way. If you're not going to gamble anymore, perhaps we can do it."

"Don't you understand, Kimberly? I have no interest in the marina. I don't want to even go there to do the mechanic's work."

"I'm willing to wait and take the chance that you'll change. It can't hurt us to wait."

But Richard shook his head. "I'm afraid it can. I haven't been paying the interest on the loan."

CHAPTER 6

The morning dawned as gray and overcast as Kimberly's spirits. Since her talk with Richard the night before, her mind had battered futilely at the problem. The idea of a second mortgage tempted her but she knew, even as the thought came to her, that it was impractical. They had to hire more help than they had now even to keep the marina operating. Repairs and upkeep had already lagged so far behind that even that would be expensive. Trying to pay off the mortgage, the back payments, and Richard's gambling debts would probably take more money than they could possibly make. And even more despairing was the knowledge that those defaulted payments had to be met, and soon.

Richard's denial that his interest in the marina would ever be revived had fallen on deaf ears. Kimberly told herself that he was suffering an overlong and twisted mourning, complicated by the drinking; it would pass. She had to believe that, for though he never admitted it, she knew he was not well enough for the hard, demanding work of a mechanic.

She knew she could fight Richard's decision to sell, or at least postpone it, but the knowledge that someone was interested in the mortgage sparked a panic she was helpless to combat. With the panic came a terrible suspicion that it was Hawke who was trying to undermine her life and her father's future. She had tried not to think about Hawke, had forced from her mind the memory of his arms about her, his lips against hers; but like the sword of Damocles, his words *I take what I want* hung in her consciousness. Would he take their marina, callously and selfishly casting them adrift with only what she could earn standing between them and stark poverty?

The cloud of worry rode down the River Road with her and hovered nearby during the day, ever ready to return when she had an idle moment. It was a bleak day, the gray sky seeming to hover close above the river that shone a dull pewter, streaked with purple-blue shadows where the moving water and slight breezes created rivulets and waves on its surface. The headlands that jutted in serried ranks into the river, tree-crowned and rock-faced, were lost in the misty distance, except for the nearest one, which brooded slate-blue and dark against the gray sky.

Kimberly noted, when she first arrived at the marina, that Hawke's boat was gone and by casual reconnoitering, she learned that Laurie Benning was not aboard her boat or anywhere about the docks. So they had gone off together. The knowledge brought a new twist of pain.

"Hello, Kimberly," a voice called, interrupting her unhappy thoughts. Looking up at the parking lot from where she stood

81

on the gravel drive, she saw Phil Bailey, a longtime customer, starting down the steps.

"You didn't pick a very good day to take off from work," she said, laughing and motioning toward the gray sky.

"It might not rain, and I see I'm not the only one." He was glancing toward the docks where several others were already underway or in the process of boarding.

Kimberly laughed. "I know. You and those others are the incurables."

Phil laughed, a boyish laugh for a man in his thirties. Looking at his handsome blondness, Kimberly wondered curiously, as she had many times before, why he had never married. He liked girls, and they certainly liked him; and although he only occasionally brought a date, he never lacked for company if he wanted it, often coming to the marina alone but inviting the daughter or sister of one of the other boat owners to join him.

"What about the regatta?" he asked. "Have you set the date yet?"

"Yes. A week from Saturday. It's on the bulletin board."

"Good. Everyone's looking forward to it."

He was obviously eager to be away, and Kimberly waved casually to him as she started up the steps to the marine store. "Have fun," she called. "And run for shelter if it starts raining. I'll open the Side Wheel and give you coffee if you get drenched."

"I'll remember that." He was off, hurrying toward where his motor sailer was moored.

Kimberly's face creased into a frown as she left him, for the regatta and the accompanying dinner dance was an expense she was loath to assume with the fate of the marina in doubt and finances in such a precarious condition. Yet it was something she could hardly avoid. Cartwright's Landing had always had a regatta in the springtime, followed by a dinner dance in the evening. Over the years the dance had become less and less informal, and for the past ten years it had been a very dressy affair, more formal than at any other marina on the river. With its old-fashioned salon the Side Wheel was the perfect setting for such an affair. Kimberly often thought that it was because of the Side Wheel salon that the dance assumed such importance. Years before, when Richard was still improving his property and business was good, he had bought a wreck of a boat, a grande dame of the rivers that had fallen on hard times and was no longer even capable of staying afloat. But its grand salon was still intact, although in sad need of repair and refurbishing. Richard had gutted it, moving not only the furnishings but the paneled walls and even the arched and carved ceiling to the

Side Wheel. It was a masterstroke of business acumen, for it had become immediately popular and brought new business to the marina – customers who spent as much time aboard the Side Wheel as they did on their own boats. Since its sale the year before, and especially since Barry had closed it except for weekends, Kimberly had watched with dread for a loss of customers. But because Barry generously allowed her to keep it open when she chose, the people had stayed – although she served nothing but coffee – and then only when the weather proved too bad for boating.

At the time of the regatta the year before, Richard had still owned the boat, but this year there would be the added expense of renting it from Barry, for they would have to have it on a weekend evening and that would mean a loss of business for him. Of course, she mused, if she had Barry's restaurant in Alton cater the dinner, it would help defray any loss he suffered. Kimberly made a mental note to speak to him about it the next time she saw him. She had already hired the band and bought the trophy for the winner.

During the dragging morning hours Kimberly was alert for the return of Hawke and Laurie, not merely with an eagerness to see Hawke but in the hope that by looking into his face, by talking to him, she would be assured that he was not the one who had inquired about the mortgage. Even he, ruthless as she was certain he was, could not smile and tease and look her honestly in the eye while he was planning their ruin.

By midafternoon the *Pandora* had not returned, but her constant watching of the river made Kimberly aware that the weather was worsening. Dark clouds shrouded the sky, and eventually a steady rain began to fall. Some of the boats on the river were already heading back to the docks. With a feeling of relief at having an excuse to leave the drudgery of the marine store, Kimberly donned a Windbreaker and a head scarf and hurried through the light rain to her boat, waving to the first arrivals as they passed and inviting them aboard the Side Wheel for coffee.

About a dozen of the boaters accepted her invitation, laughing as they hurried into the salon, shaking water from their hair and clothes and hanging Windbreakers and raincoats on a convenient hall tree, not at all dismayed at the interruption of their outings.

"You never should have sold this steamer," Phil Bailey told her. "It just isn't the same when we can't come here whenever we want to. The place has a charm that belongs more to the past than the present. It's fascinating."

85

Kimberly smiled and nodded in agreement. "I'll have the coffee for you soon," she told them as they gathered around the tables.

"Is that all you have?" one of the men asked. "Something a little stronger might be appreciated. We're all wet and in need of something medicinal."

"You know that's all I have," Kimberly told him, laughing. "But if any of you has something medicinal, you're welcome to bring it aboard. I have ice and Mr. Mead has soda."

Several of the men hurried back out into the rain, promising to be gone only a minute, and Kimberly brought cups, glasses, and a bowl of ice from the kitchen.

"This room is magnificent," one of the women said as Kimberly placed the ice bowl on the table. "These must have been the original furnishings."

As Kimberly explained to her about the original *River Queen,* the woman's eyes moved about the salon, alight with interest.

"Of course it was a much larger salon," Kimberly told her. "The boat it came from was far larger than the Side Wheel, so only part of it could be used. But it is impressive, isn't it?"

Kimberly herself never tired of looking at the ornate room. It was necessarily long for its width, as had been the original

86

salon from which it came. The walls were paneled walnut but little of them showed, for between the rows of windows on either side of the room were long pier-glass mirrors in elaborate gilt frames that gave a spacious look to the room. The walls rose to meet a vaulted, groined ceiling alive with carvings, most of which were of flowers, leaves, and vines. In the vaults of the ceiling, between the carved groins, were sunbursts formed of plaster, and from the center of each sunburst hung a chain supporting one of the massive brass chandeliers, eight of which hung in a straight line down the center of the room, clustered with milk-glass globes from which lamp chimneys protruded, although they were now electrified. The original carpeting had been a luxuriously thick wool with a floral design, but it had been almost unrecognizable as such when Richard bought the boat. In consideration of practicality Richard had replaced it with indoor-outdoor carpeting, also with a floral design in shades of maroon, rose and blue. A center aisle opened down the middle of the salon, on each side of which was a double row of marble-top walnut tables supported by a cluster of carved legs. These, too, were from the old steamer.

Only at the far end of the room had the decor been changed. A low platform had been built for musicians and before it a dance floor, not large, but still able to accommodate a reasonable number of couples.

"We don't really seem to fit in this room, do we?" the woman said. "I mean, look at us in our shorts and ... well." She laughed, moving her hand to indicate the formal setting.

"No," Kimberly agreed. "We don't seem to belong. But when we have the dance after the regatta, we do."

"Oh." The woman's face brightened. "You have a dance? I hadn't heard about it."

"Is this your first time here?" Kimberly asked, aware that she had never seen the woman before.

"Yes. I'm Martha Lansing. I'm with the Coreys."

Kimberly introduced herself and then hurried to the kitchen for the coffee. The men had returned with their bottles. One of them was mixing drinks, the other passing them around.

"How about you, Kimberly?" called Ray Corey. "Will you have a drink?"

"Thanks, but I'll stay with the coffee," she told him as she turned on the chandelier nearest where they sat. Despite the many windows, the room was dim as twilight.

It was a pleasant few hours, and Kimberly

would have enjoyed herself completely if thoughts of Hawke had not intruded, causing her to glance often toward the windows on the river side of the boat for a sight of the *Pandora* returning to the dock.

Finally Phil Bailey said, "If we take too much advantage of Kimberly, she might not open the salon the next time we get rained off the river, so let's not overstay our welcome."

"You're always welcome," Kimberly told them, but she was not unhappy to see them gathering their things and preparing to leave amid many thanks for her hospitality.

Kimberly tidied the room, then, after turning off the lights and locking the door, she stood undecided. The idea of returning to the marine store and her desk work was repugnant, yet she was reluctant to go home without seeing Hawke. Glancing at the sky, she noted that it was still dull and sullen, but the rain had stopped. There would be an early dusk, but it was still hours before nightfall, and with sudden determination she climbed down into her boat and headed back to the marine store to change her clothes. She would seek her usual panacea: a trip to one of the islands in search of driftwood.

Ten minutes later Kimberly was stepping into her boat, tossing the canvas carrier and a Windbreaker onto the seat beside her. She was reaching for the tie rope, ready to cast off, when movement on the dock caught her eye, and she looked up to see Hawke coming toward her. At the sudden sight of him her face broke into a welcome smile that she quickly subdued, remembering her suspicions about him and resentful that he had spent his day with Laurie. But she had not been quick enough to hide her pleasure in seeing him and something flashed deep in his eyes before he grinned back at her. For the moment her doubts and suspicions were forgotten, and there was only the thump of her heart and a tingling awareness of him.

"Are we off on another profitable venture in search of driftwood?"

"I am. Although I really don't much care if I find any. I just wanted to be alone on one of the islands."

"Is it absolutely necessary that you be alone?" he asked leaning toward her, his black eyes probing hers.

She forced herself not to look away as she answered, but when he looked at her like that, he seemed to lay bare all her secret thoughts and yearnings.

"You're welcome to come," she said, hearing the husky breathiness of her own voice.

He stepped easily and gracefully into the

bobbing boat, balancing himself against the movement, then reached past her to cast off, and sitting down, pushed hard against the dock to move the boat out into the harbor.

When they cleared the point, Kimberly turned the boat upstream. Here the breeze was brisker, already whipping and snapping her hair back from her face, although they had not yet reached full speed, and she lifted her head, savoring the coolness of the misty air that held the damp scent of the river. Opposite her, Hawke's dark eyes studied her until she became uncomfortably aware of his scrutiny. With a feeling of relief she saw him glance questioningly toward an island she was bypassing. She smiled, shaking her head, for she had already determined to go to a larger island farther up the river.

The roar of the motor precluded conversation, and in this enforced silence Kimberly's mind was busy; alone with him on an island she might somehow bring the conversation around to the marina. Then, during the talk, she could suggest subtly that he buy half the marina. They could be partners, or at least he and Richard could be partners, and until Richard was ready to assume control again, she could manage it for them. And then, her treacherous heart seemed to whisper, *He can't go forever out of my life.*

The large island Kimberly headed for had a submerged sandbar extending almost two hundred feet from its downriver side, where the propeller could easily snag, so as she usually did, she skirted it and approached from its head, where a beach sloped steeply into the water. Here she brought the boat about, running its prow into the sand to ground it while the outboard hung free in the deep water beyond.

"We'll have to crawl out over the prow," she told Hawke. "Unless, of course, you want another dunking."

"It's too cool for a dunking this evening," he said, handing her her Windbreaker and getting into his own. "Give me your hand so you won't fall in."

When they stood side by side on the beach, he still held her hand cupped in his as he gazed around.

"Why this particular island?" he asked. "Does it have something to offer that those we passed lack?"

"Well, it's larger and it catches more driftwood. But I really like it because the trees in the center are big and spreading and there's hardly any underbrush. Most of these islands are so overgrown, you can hardly walk anywhere but along the beaches."

"Then you don't just come out to collect driftwood."

"Oh, I guess I'm like these men who go hunting and never shoot anything. Going hunting is just their excuse or reason for getting out and away from things. Most men don't like to say they just went for a walk in the woods to enjoy nature."

"I didn't know you were such an authority on men and their likes and dislikes." There was a teasing note in his voice and a smile on his face as he looked down at her. His hand was warm against her own. Suddenly Kimberly was aware of how alone they were on this tiny beach in the wide expanse of the river. It was almost as if they were the only people in a great wilderness, just the two of them alone together. But the soft, warm feeling died, washed away by the memory of her distrust. Even now, while she was being so foolishly romantic, he might have already set in motion plans that would destroy her hopes for the future.

"Let's look for driftwood," she said, drawing her hand from his and walking away down the beach.

Keeping easy pace with her, he was silent for several moments. Then he said, his voice calm but his words evenly spaced, "I was not referring to the other evening."

93

She looked at him in surprise, having forgotten in her flight of fancy what it was he had said.

"Oh, I was thinking about something else," she said when his words came back to her.

"Then I was right in the first place. You don't know much about men or you would realize it's very wounding to the ego to have a woman's thoughts somewhere else when she's with you."

This time she laughed. "Nothing could wound your ego; it's invulnerable."

"But I have a softer side to my nature too."

She looked at him searchingly. Was this just banter or was he being frank and outspoken as he sometimes was? She was unaware of the hope in her clear amber eyes as she thought that, if there was a softer side to his nature, perhaps he would be open to her suggestion that he buy half the marina.

But he seemed to misread that look of hope, for his arms were suddenly around her, drawing her close, bending above her as his lips sought hers. Kimberly submitted meekly to his kiss while sirens of alarm shrieked in her mind, warning her not to surrender to the sudden assault on her senses, not to be lost again in the magic of his embrace. But her heart beat madly and when he released her,

her breath came in short gasps that she tried to hide from him.

If he was as moved as she was, there was no outward show, for, taking her hand again, he said casually, "Let's look at your forest primeval instead of collecting driftwood."

They walked on the leaf-strewn ground beneath the towering trees hand in hand as Kimberly tried to match his easy camaraderie and disguise her soaring happiness at having him here beside her.

It was dim under the trees, and they had no view of the river through the circling undergrowth. Not until a particularly strong gust of wind churned through the upper branches of the tall trees were they warned that the weather was changing.

"We had better see what's happening out there," Hawke said, leading the way toward the narrow, twisting path through the underbrush where they had entered the woods.

They stepped onto the beach into a building current of wind that swept down the river. Gone was the pale-gray overcast, lost in a churning mass rumbling down from the northwest; the first roll of thunder ended in a loud crash. As they dashed toward the head of the island the rain started, a few spattering drops that quickly turned into a torrential downpour. They were drenched by

95

the time they turned at the end of the island and stopped, staring in disbelief at the empty beach where the boat had been grounded. The wind-driven water churned and billowed, splashing up white-crested wavelets over the surface of the river and sweeping strongly up the beach. Far out in the main channel they could see the small boat twisting and turning as it swept swiftly downstream.

Kimberly shivered with the chill that was coming into the darkening air. Her Windbreaker was not waterproof, and the cold rain, already soaking through to her skin, ran in rivulets inside her wet clothes.

"We'll have to find some shelter before it's too dark to see," Hawke shouted above the storm.

Shelter? Kimberly thought. *What shelter?* There was no shelter on the island other than the trees. But Hawke already had her hand and was hurrying her back the way they had come. He thrashed through the narrow path in the undergrowth, and led her through the trees to the far side of the open woods, where a downed tree lay partially buried in undergrowth. There, beneath the trees, he stamped out a clearing under a full, sprawling bush. The wind barely penetrated this spot, and Hawke drew Kimberly down beside him in a space so small that there was barely

96

room for both of them. It seemed almost silent in comparison to the raging gale on the outer perimeter of the island, and in the lessening noise the sound of Kimberly's chattering teeth clicked like castanets, for the air was becoming colder.

Hawke reached out a hand to touch her trembling arm. "Take off that jacket," he told her. "It's not doing you any good."

Obediently she removed the jacket.

"The shirt too."

"No!" The T-shirt might be wet but it was better than nothing.

"Take it off. I want you to put on this jacket. It's waterproof," he said, already unzipping it and struggling out of it in the narrow, confined place where he sat between the tree and one of its branches.

Chilled to the bone, she quickly slipped out of the T-shirt. When her trembling fingers fumbled with the zipper, Hawke brushed them aside and zipped the jacket for her. Then, rising to one knee, he picked her up in his arms and settled back in the angle of the tree with Kimberly on his lap, his arms drawing her close. With one hand he pressed her face into the hollow of his neck and with the other vigorously massaged her back.

The Windbreaker had kept his shirt dry, and Kimberly leaned close against his warmth as the chill that gripped her shook her entire body. Despite his closeness and the friction of his massage, she continued to shake, feeling that her bones themselves were frozen and sending waves of cold through her that radiated to her wet, clammy skin. She felt Hawke's hand slip down and under the Windbreaker, and it felt deliciously hot against her chilled back. Again he rubbed, the hard, sweeping strokes catching on her bra until he fumblingly loosened its clasp. Slowly, the violent shaking eased until it was no more than a tremor, and Kimberly breathed deeply in long, quick breaths, realizing that she had been gasping shallowly through clenched teeth in her effort to control the racking chill.

CHAPTER 7

While in the grip of the chill Kimberly had been too miserable to think of anything but the warmth Hawke afforded. Aware of him, yes; knowing in her mind that his arms held her, but not emotionally involved. Now this intimacy flooded her awareness. She could feel the beat of his heart against her, his arms close and protecting, his hands – stilled now – but warm against the bare skin of her back. His neck was straight and hard against her cheek, and her lips touched his throat. Although her own arms were loosely about him, she held very still, listening to his heartbeat, fearful that any action on her part might reveal to him the terrible yearning that was beginning to rise in her, the tingling happiness she felt at being alone with him. Through her mind went all the reasons why she disliked and distrusted him, and she tried to shore up her dislike by calling to mind all the times he had angered her. Above all, she concentrated on the threat he was to Richard, and consequently to herself. But at this moment it was very hard to sustain that hatred, knowing, as she did, that despite everything she had fallen in love with him.

A raindrop running down his neck coursed along Kimberly's nose and fell to her lips, causing her to flick out her tongue in an almost reflex action that Hawke felt immediately. Lifting his head slightly, he tried to peer down at her in the darkness.

"I thought you were asleep."

"Maybe I was," Kimberly said, not quite lying, as she lifted her arms to brace her hands against the tree trunk and push away from him.

"No. Stay here; it's so cold, you might get

another chill." His voice was bland, casual, as he drew her close to him again.

She lay quietly for long moments, trying to still the clamor of her heart, feeling the wet discomfort of her rain-soaked jeans, listening to the wild battering of the rain as it crashed through the foliage above them. The violent sounds of the storm seemed to cut them off from the rest of the world as much as the wide river flowing all around the empty island. They were alone here, as if the rest of the world no longer existed.

Then Hawke bent his head, and she felt his lips on her forehead. His hands on her back moved, not massaging but caressing. She went rigidly still and then slowly, almost as if against her will, she lifted her head. His lips traveled along her temple, down her cheek, moving gently until they found her mouth. Then he crushed her to him, his lips firm but gentle as he held her in a long embrace. Kimberly sighed almost with relief as the terrible tension eased, and her arms closed around him. His lips moved from hers, trailing down her neck to the curve of her shoulder. Kimberly felt his warm breath inside the neck of the jacket, flowing caressingly over her chilled skin and sending a thrill tingling all the way down to her toes.

"You're a little passionflower," he

murmured, and his words broke the spell. Suddenly this was cheap, common, having nothing to do with love. She felt that he would have acted so no matter who he held in his arms. For him this was just a romantically opportune moment – of which he would take full advantage – not the tearingly ardent, once-in-a-lifetime experience it was for her.

"I'm not," she said, pulling slightly away from him, turning her head to avoid his lips. Disappointment in him swamped her, and for a moment it was not hard to hate him for not loving her. And then the thought came to her: why not use this moment to her own advantage? But she had to let him know that she would go so far and no further. Leaning away from him slightly, she put her hands on his arms, pushing them down and away so that they were no longer under the jacket caressing her bare back. Then she again leaned against him.

"It's just the romance of being stranded on a desert island," she murmured, wary and distrustful now, cool and calculating, the treacherous emotions he could arouse in her clamped down under a new determination.

He chuckled, gathering her again into his arms. "If you want to call it romance, then we'll call it romance."

Her arms crept up around his neck as she

returned his kiss, one hand tangled in his wet hair, half of her mind whirling with the problem of how to approach the suggestion that he buy half of the marina, the other half coldly forbidding her to succumb to his gentle lovemaking. When he tried to move his hands under the jacket, again she gently pushed away from him, only to relax once more in his arms saying, "Tell me about yourself, Hawke. I don't know very much about you."

"There isn't much to tell."

"Well, there must be something. You didn't just happen when you arrived at Cartwright's Landing."

The wind and rain had lessened, and they no longer had to raise their voices to be heard above it, but the night continued chill.

"I'm in the marina business because I found a way of life I like, and I decided to make it more than just something for free moments. What I do for a living many men can do only for pleasure. I guess I'm like your father in that way."

"But he only has one marina. He was never successful the way you are. How did you get into the business?"

"I was in college studying to be an engineer, and hating it. I picked engineering because if I was successful, I could at least be outdoors when I was building roads or bridges, but the paperwork was anathema. Then an aunt I hardly knew died and left me some money. It was a lot of money for someone who didn't have any, but not enough to be independently wealthy, and that's what I wanted to be. I used the money to buy a marina. The man who owned it was old and had arthritis and couldn't work any longer. I worked for him first, took over so much of the work that he was finally dependent on me, and then I asked to buy half interest. He didn't really want to sell, but with me as a partner he knew he wouldn't have to bother with anything, just leave it all for me to handle. Since I was working and he wasn't, I had a salary too. It was a good marina, and within two years I was able to buy him out."

"Did he want to sell?" Kimberly asked, thinking that the deal sounded slightly unscrupulous.

"Not really. But he eventually saw it my way."

"How did that happen?"

"I don't know if I would have been a good engineer or not, but I'm a very good businessman."

He means he's a ruthless businessman, Kimberly thought, and wondered how he could speak of it so casually, without seeming to feel any compunction about revealing what to her was a moral lack.

"After that it was just a matter of carefully investing what I had saved until I could buy another marina. Finally there was enough money so that there was no need to save; when I found something worth buying, I bought it. Now I can afford to be a bum."

Yes, Kimberly thought, he's ruthless. As he once said, he takes what he wants. He would take her too if he could, but he was wise enough to know that was impossible. She shivered slightly, wondering if it would be impossible if there was no Richard and no marina to stand between them and make him her enemy.

"You're still cold?" he asked, gathering her closer in his arms.

"No. I was just thinking, Hawke. Why can't you buy half interest in our marina? I could run it until Richard is able to take over again. It – it" – she stumbled over the words, hating to admit that it was only because of Richard's gambling that she had had to let it get so run-down – "it doesn't look the way it does because of poor management; I just couldn't put the money it earned back into the business."

He was silent for so long that she thought he was considering her suggestion, and when

104

he finally spoke, she was startled at the quiet anger in his low voice. "Is that the reason you've been so obliging? Were the soft kisses, the controlled passion all an act?" His voice hardened. "Did I stop too soon? How far would you have been willing to go to save your precious marina for your drunken father?"

Suddenly his hands were rough on her shoulders, dragging her to him as his mouth came down on hers in a punishing kiss. Then his weight was forcing her backward onto the ground. His silent rage was terrifying in the black darkness, and Kimberly wished she could see his face as she tried to fight him off. But he pinned her down as he leaned over her.

"Tell me, Kimberly. How far would you have gone?"

"Let me go, Hawke," she said through clenched teeth, trying not to let him know how frightened she was.

The long blast of a foghorn cut through the night air, freezing them both for a moment. Then a sweeping light brightened the mist gleaming beyond the undergrowth. Kimberly felt the pressure of his hands on her shoulders lessen and heard his breath come in a ragged sigh.

"They must be looking for us," she said

in a voice weak with relief, but Hawke was already on his feet, calling, moving through the darkness toward the light. Another blast of the foghorn drowned out his voice. Kimberly tried to follow him, but he was lost in the darkness, and she could only move slowly toward the gleam of misty air that showed in pale patches between the trees, indicating the open river beyond the tall brush. When she forced her way through the surrounding bushes to the narrow beach, the boat was gone, lost in the mist, only its sweeping light glowing dimly. Hawke stood farther up the beach at the edge of the water looking after it.

"They'll be back, or there might be another along," he told her. "We'll have to stay here so they can see us." His voice was normal again, the anger gone. "If we can find a place to wait in the undergrowth, we'll be out of the breeze."

As he spoke he moved toward the bushes. Uncertainly Kimberly followed him, for she was shivering again in the faint breeze that came down the river, a breeze too light to clear the mist that hung damply to her face, but strong enough to make her wet jeans and dripping hair feel icy.

"Here's a good spot," Hawke said, pushing aside some bushes.

Kimberly hesitated. Although there was no

anger in his voice, and he acted as if he had completely forgotten the episode that had been interrupted by the arrival of the boat, she was uncertain. He had frightened her badly.

"Come on, Kimberly."

Hesitantly she moved toward him. She could hardly stand out here and freeze, but it seemed childish to seek out a spot for herself. She ached in every muscle, thinking it must be the result of that terrible chill, and knew she needed more shelter than was provided by a few bushes.

As she neared him he reached for her arm. "Stop being silly," he said. "You might be getting pneumonia already. Now sit down. What is that you have in your hand?"

Kimberly glanced down. She could not recall picking up her T-shirt and jacket, and wondered how she had even found them in the dark, but there they were in her hand.

"I can sit on them," she told him.

"They're wetter than the ground where I brushed the leaves away." He indicated the spot, and she sat down obediently.

Her arms clamped around her knees, Kimberly sat staring at the misty river, feeling her muscles tense with cold and her teeth begin to chatter. Hawke reached for her. "I can't let you die of the cold," he said, drawing her close to him. Reluctantly she let herself be drawn into his embrace, more fearful of another chill than of Hawke, whose anger seemed to have passed. For a long time they sat with his arms holding her close, but it was such an impersonal embrace that Kimberly perversely began to resent it. If she were a bag of laundry, she thought, he could hardly be less aware of her. Yet she had no wish to repeat the scene that had occurred back in the woods. Finally, when she had decided the silence would last forever, he said, "Don't ever try to use me again, Kimberly. I promise you, it won't be safe. Did you actually think you could lure me into buying a partnership?" When she did not answer, he shook her slightly. "Did you?"

"Why not?" she said, flaring at him angrily. "You use people, don't you?"

"Only when I know I have control of the situation. You're too much of a novice to try it; you could have lost everything and gained nothing. But you didn't ever intend to lose everything, did you?"

"No," she told him pointedly.

"You hold yourself in high esteem. You thought a few kisses would do it."

"No. I thought you were intelligent enough

108

to see that it would be a very good business move. I was mistaken." She pulled away from him, glowering into his dark, shadowed face, indignant at his belittling remarks. "And I have reason to hold myself in high esteem. There's nothing in my life for me to be ashamed of, and I don't think that's something you can honestly claim."

"Perhaps I can't, but while you're holding yourself in such high esteem, remember those of us who aren't so honorable always have the upper hand over virtue and kindness. Why should I be willing to share something with a hopeless drunk and gambler when I can have it all to myself? No scruples stand in my way, and I told you before, I take what I want if I can get it."

There was a tone in his voice that seemed to suggest he meant more than just the marina.

CHAPTER 8

An hour later another boat, its lights flashing along the shores of the islands, found them. Back at the marina all the lights gleamed bright in the dark mist of the river.

Richard, his face drawn with worry, welcomed Kimberly with open arms, Mrs. Kramer at his side. Mr. Glass, the night watchman, was there, along with Barry, several boat owners who lived nearby, and some unfamiliar faces. At the edge of the crowd stood Laurie Benning, watching with narrowed eyes as Kimberly was helped onto the dock, trailed by Hawke.

"Kitten, you scared us to death. Thank God you're all right," Richard said, hugging her to him.

"My boat washed away in the storm," she told him. "We were all right except for the cold and rain. We were on an island."

"Don't stand there talking, Richard Cartwright," Mrs. Kramer said. "The poor thing is frozen. Here, give me that." She lifted the bundled jacket and T-shirt from Kimberly's hand, glanced at it to see if something was rolled in the wet folds, shoved it at Richard and led Kimberly to the car.

Mrs. Kramer's prescription for exposure was a stiff drink of whiskey that left Kimberly choking and gasping; a scaldingly hot bath; and three hot-water bottles warming the bed, where she tucked the protesting girl under layers of blankets.

"Now, I don't want you too warm, so we can take off some of those blankets as soon as

110

you feel comfortable," she said, in her glory at being at the center of the excitement.

"I feel too warm now," Kimberly told her, although the heat did seem to draw away some of the soreness from her muscles, which ached as if she had spent a long day at gruelingly hard labor.

"All right, I'll take one off." She seated herself beside the bed. "Now tell me all about it."

Richard and Barry had been banished to another part of the house while Mrs. Kramer was helping Kimberly, and the woman obviously had no intention of leaving until her curiosity was satisfied.

"There isn't much to tell. How did you discover we were lost so soon?"

"Well, it wasn't hard. When you didn't come home, Richard called Barry, and when he hadn't seen you, he called me and then Mr. Glass. Mr. Glass saw you leave and didn't think anything of it until Richard called him. Then when he checked, and your boat was missing, we got some of the local people to look for you. How did you lose your boat?"

"It was washed away while we were on the island. Then we just waited."

"Oh, Kimberly, I do declare, you're impossible. Such a romantic adventure, and with

111

a handsome man like Mr. Hawke, and you couldn't care less. Why, what could be more romantic than being cast away on a desert island?"

Suddenly Mrs. Kramer seemed struck by an unwelcome thought. "Kimberly! He isn't married, is he?"

"No, he isn't married. Mrs. Kramer, do you mind if I go to sleep? I feel dreadfully tired."

Having learned nothing, she was obviously reluctant to leave.

"Of course not, but we can talk about it tomorrow," she said, cheering herself. "Do you want me to take some of these covers off?"

"Please. And thank you so much."

As tired as she was, Kimberly lay in the darkness, taking comfort in the knowledge that Hawke thought the only reason for her ardent response to his lovemaking was to lure him into investing in the marina. And God keep him from ever knowing that it was anything else, she thought, for if he even suspected that his very touch made her heart leap and her blood rush madly, she would be at his mercy. Oh, he was loathsome, she told herself, but she turned her head into the pillow, her eyes hot with tears. No matter how loathsome she assured herself he was, it did nothing to stop the terrible yearning she felt when she thought of him, and she seemed to be always thinking of him.

Kimberly awoke to the sound of birdsong and brilliant daylight late the next day. At her first movement every muscle in her body seemed to shriek in agony, so that she edged cautiously from the bed, tottering like a very old woman, when she finally gained her feet. Was this the result of exposure, she wondered, or had that chill caused all this soreness? She longed for a leisurely hot bath, but her stomach rumbled menacingly and a wave of dizziness swept over her. Hungry as she was, she was uncertain that her wobbling legs would carry her down the steps, so she decided she would settle for a short hot bath.

The hot water proved so beneficial, seeming to draw away the myriad aches and pains, that it was forty-five minutes later when she drew on a deep-blue robe and went down for a late breakfast. Although Richard was obviously not home, she brushed away the grate of anxiety that came with the thought that he might again be drinking, his worry about her the night before being the excuse. She was too hungry at the moment to think of anything but food, and besides, what could she do about it anyway?

She was loitering over her second cup of coffee when the door knocker clattered, and she opened it to find Hawke waiting on the porch, an alert, questioning look on his dark face. Since she had awakened, the memory of the night before had been with her; not the harsh anger nor ugly disagreements but the tender moments when he had kissed her gently and held her near. Those thoughts were so close to the surface of her mind now, that she felt a warmth rising in her face at the sight of him and hoped it was not showing in a blush.

"Well, am I invited in or do we stand here and talk?" he asked.

"Oh, yes, come in. I was just having coffee. Would you care for some?"

"Thank you."

Kimberly led the way to the kitchen, noticing as she put another blue cup and saucer on the table and poured coffee, that Hawke stood studying the room, obviously interested.

"This room is perfect," he finally said. "It fits the town."

"It's been part of the village since the beginning," Kimberly told him. "Even some of the furniture, although it's older than the house."

"How old is the village?"

114

"It was founded in the 1850s." She was beginning to wonder why he had come. Surely not to discuss the village and look at the house.

"I've only seen it when I was driving through to come here. I'd like to walk around, really get the flavor of it." He sat down at the table and his dark eyes came to rest on her, studying her face, noting the robe, and then coming back to her face again. It was a wraparound robe, belted at the waist and, under the keen appraisal of his black eyes, Kimberly checked the neckline to assure herself it had not loosened and fallen open. She was suddenly conscious of the fact that she was wearing nothing under it. She got out of the chair, carefully holding the front of the robe closed. "Will you excuse me while I dress?" she asked, moving toward the door without waiting for an answer.

She heard his chuckle as she went from the room and knew he had noted her embarrassment and was probably aware of the reason for it.

Although her mind was full of Hawke, the need for deciding on something to wear brought her thoughts to more immediate matters, and with a start she realized that it was Saturday, one of the busiest days at the marina. Hastily she dressed, drew a comb

115

through her hair, dashed on some lipstick, and hurried back down the stairs.

"I just realized it's Saturday," she told Hawke when she reached the kitchen. "I have to go to the marina."

"Sit down. Your father is holding down the fort beautifully."

"You mean he's working?" she asked in amazement.

"He's giving every indication of it. Somebody found your boat and brought it back. They said it was down at the dam. He's checking it for damage and changing the propeller. One of the blades was bent."

"I told you he only needed time and he would go back to work," Kimberly told him as if her point had been made.

But Hawke said nothing, merely giving her a sardonic grin. As her brows flew together in anger, he raised a hand, his palm toward her to stop her words. "Let's not argue today," he suggested. "I really came to learn how you were feeling. Since you obviously don't have pneumonia, will you take a walk with me?"

Slightly appeased, Kimberly agreed, for she was always happy to show people Elsah, having a proprietary pride in the village that was her home.

Besides the shadows cast by the two tall bluffs on either side of the village, the ancient

116

trees spread their limbs high above the second stories of the houses, adding their own shade to the streets. Dappled sunlight fell on the couple as they walked along beneath the trees, brightening the pale yellow of Kimberly's slacks and blouse and catching blue gleams in Hawke's dark hair. Many of the houses were extremely small, built of mellowed stone with frame additions strung to the sides and rear, but there was a good representation of two-story homes as well – some stone, others brick – but all old, beautifully kept, and few with more than a tiny patch of lawn. Even the most recently built houses had the dignity of years, although they did not date back to the middle of the last century. From every part of the village one or both of the protecting bluffs could be seen, their steep brush-clad sides crowding close.

Hawke admired the village, listened with interest as Kimberly related snatches of history, and they laughed together at the lettering on one huge frame building. Faded but still clearly legible were the words WAGONS AND BUGGIES MADE AND REPAIRED.

"It gives you the feeling you've stepped back in time," Hawke said.

"Yes, it does," Kimberly agreed. "But I never realized it until I came home after being away at college." Her face was alight with pleasure. Not only did Hawke appreciate the village she loved so well, but the easy friendliness between them, when she had thought there could be nothing but enmity, affected her like a strong drink, intoxicating her with happiness.

The artists, several of whom had set up easels at advantageous positions, occasioned Hawke's comment.

"We're so used to them, we hardly notice," Kimberly told him.

"They add a Greenwich Village touch to the town," Hawke said. Then, shaking his head, he added, "You just don't expect to find a town like this in the Mid-west. I'm surprised more hasn't been done to commercialize it. It has an unusual charm."

"It's become bad enough," Kimberly said with disapproval. "Look at all this traffic. It's like this every weekend now. It used to be quiet and peaceful, but that was before there was so much publicity."

"Traffic?" Hawke glanced at the few cars that occasionally passed. "You can hardly call it conjested."

"Well, you have to look before you cross the street now, and it never used to be like that."

"You're opposed to progress. I'm

wondering if there isn't some way to make this town pay. It's wasted the way it is."

Kimberly stared at him in shocked dismay. "Make Elsah pay?"

"It needs promotion, but the promoter would have to see profit to make it worthwhile. I just wonder what could be done."

"You mean how it can be ruined. Hawke, if I thought you could turn Elsah into one of those hideous tourist attractions, all commercial and crowded, with fat women in short shorts, I'd never speak to you again." The very idea of anyone tampering with Elsah infuriated her.

But Hawke merely smiled and asked, "Do you have to call me Hawke? My name is Christopher – Chris to friends."

"I didn't know we were friends. Besides, I think Hawke suits you perfectly – hovering around, destructive, a thief."

"Aren't you referring to a crow?"

"Whatever it is, there is nothing you can do to commercialize Elsah, thank God. Your money won't do you any good because it's been named a Historic District, and that means you can't tamper with it. It has to remain as it is."

"Too bad," was all he said, not seeming in the least disappointed, and Kimberly looked at him closely, wondering if he had said all this merely to anger her.

"Why are you so impossible? Why can't you be nice?"

"Because it's so much more entertaining to see you angry than to just have dull, prosaic conversation. It adds a little spice to relationships, don't you think?"

"I might think so if I weren't always the one doing the entertaining." But there was no heat in her voice, and she ducked her head so that he would not see the curve of her smile.

CHAPTER 9

Saturday was a busy day at the marina, the boaters usually staying on the water until nightfall, after which many of them gathered in the Side Wheel for a late dinner and hours of visiting. It was too long a day for Richard, Kimberly decided, so by four o'clock she was at the marina ready to relieve him, thinking he was probably in need of rest. The hot bath and the exercise, combined with the long night's sleep, had healed all the ravages of the evening before, and she felt rested and ready to go back to work.

The sun was brilliant on the wide stretch of river, where there was a busy coming and going of every kind of craft. Gazing at the docks, Kimberly saw that most of the slips were empty, which meant that once all the weekend crowd was afloat, Richard had not been interrupted by constant demands on his time, and had been free to do whatever work he chose in comparative peace.

She found him in the marine store seated at the desk, the chair tilted back, his feet up, obviously taking a much needed rest.

"You go on home, Dad," she told him. "I can stay for the rest of the evening."

"You're feeling all right then?" There was a shadow of worry in his eyes.

"I'm fine."

"I didn't want to call. I was afraid I'd wake you. You're sure you feel good enough to stay?"

"I'm fine. You just go on."

"I will, then. I forgot how to work, I guess. By the way, I put one of the boys to painting that boat in the shed."

"I forgot all about it! Was the paint gun ruined?"

"No. Jimmy found it and cleaned it. He's a good boy."

At the door he turned. "I almost forgot. Barry was looking for you, and that Miss

121

Benning wants to talk to you. She was here earlier, and I said I could help her, but she said to ask you to come over if you came in."

He stopped in the doorway, turning back and looking at her wryly. "You know, Kitten, you were right. I should have been back working before this. It was like – well, not exactly old times, but, well, I'm beat and I still feel good. I enjoyed being here." Then his face fell as he said, "It's a shame I waited too late to find out."

"It's not too late. It's never too late. We'll find a way. I know we will."

But he shook his head. "I don't think we will. Not in time."

She watched him through the window as he walked toward his car. Kimberly's heart twisted as she noted the discouraged droop in his shoulders, the slow drag of his feet. Why, he looked like an old man! *No,* she thought, *I won't let him lose everything. I'll find some way to save the marina for him.* He's tired now and discouraged, but if he had hope, if he could have things as they had once been, the life would come back to his step, he would work again and find a way to pick up his life from where he had dropped it three years ago. But Hawke was the only hope, the only one who could help them, and Hawke had already refused her once. A tremor ran through her as she recalled his violent anger when he warned her never to try to use him, that it wouldn't be safe if she ever tried again. But she refused to give up hope.

Kimberly had no wish to see Laurie Benning but at least she would be spared watching her languid possessiveness with Hawke, for after leaving her earlier, he had gone into Alton. After he announced that he was going there, Kimberly had at first been frantic at the idea that it might be to take over the mortgage on the marina. Then she had realized that the bank would be closed at that hour on Saturday.

Well, she could hardly refuse to see Laurie. It would be poor business to do so, because they needed the money from the rental of the slip where her father's yacht was moored. In addition Kimberly had to admit to a certain curiosity, for there was no reason she could think of for Laurie to want to see her.

"Come aboard," Laurie called gaily, having seen Kimberly coming along the gravel drive.

Kimberly mounted the steep steps up the side of the tall yacht, noting that Laurie wore a halter top and very short shorts that displayed her elegantly long legs, now tanned to a pale gold. Laurie's lush elegance made Kimberly feel scrawny and unattractive, but she knew it was more her relationship to

123

Hawke that roused the jealousy and bitter resentment she always felt at the sight of the girl. At the moment Laurie was obviously using all her powers to charm – her red lips smiling, her very attitude dripping with welcome – but they did nothing to dispel Kimberly's dislike for her.

"Will you have a drink?" she asked when Kimberly reached the deck.

"No, thank you. My father said you wanted to see me."

"I do. I think we should get to know each other better." The smile was less bright than it had been.

"I really haven't time to visit today. Is there something you want?"

"Yes." Now the smile was entirely gone, replaced by a sincere gaze. "I think we should talk."

Kimberly was instantly alert. There could be only one subject Laurie might want to discuss with her: Hawke.

"I guess we can talk," she agreed, too curious now to refuse.

"Let's go into the cabin; it's more comfortable there. And even if you don't want a drink, I think I'll have one."

The cabin was large, all mahogany and brass with greenish gold fabric covering the

124

furniture and at the ports, but Kimberly was hardly aware of it, so intent was she on Laurie.

"That was very clever of you to get yourself shipwrecked," Laurie said as she mixed a drink, her back to Kimberly.

"It was hardly clever. We almost froze," Kimberly told her, ignoring Laurie's implication.

Laurie turned, a bright, taunting smile on her lips as she moved to one of the chairs and sank gracefully into it, crossing her lovely legs, swirling the ice in her glass – and all the while regarding Kimberly as if waiting for a denial that she had purposely found a way to shipwreck them. When Kimberly remained silent, her face composed in a bland expression, Laurie was forced to take up the conversation herself.

"I don't know you very well – is it Kimberly?" At Kimberly's nod she continued. "Well, I don't know you very well, but I do know girls like you. You're probably more clever than some of the others, but the results were the same. You see, I know what happened on that island."

Kimberly nodded calmly. "I suppose Hawke told you."

"Chris didn't have to tell me anything; I saw you when you came back." She laughed.

125

"What were you trying to do, advertise it by carrying your blouse and jacket?"

Kimberly's eyebrows rose, but she kept her face bland, refusing to show the anger and disgust she was feeling, yet interested to see where the conversation was leading.

"I would have known anyway, of course, because I know Chris," Laurie continued.

Something about the way she said "Chris" grated on Kimberly, for it made him seem to belong to Laurie.

"But I guess you know for yourself by now that he takes anything he can get."

"I'm afraid I don't know him that well. You might be aware from personal experience what he does or doesn't do, but you can hardly claim to know me as well." Kimberly's cool, superior tone was calculated to anger Laurie, as was the faintly smiling attitude that she hoped concealed her growing anger.

Now Laurie's delicately refined features hardened as she stared at Kimberly with open dislike.

"Don't pretend with me," she said in a hard, accusing voice. "I've seen it happen before. The dumb little girl lures him into a compromising position, hoping she can get something out of it – marriage, preferably. And why not? He's not only handsome, he's rich. Only what the poor little girl doesn't

126

realize until too late is that Chris Hawke can't be compromised." She ended on a note of jeering satisfaction.

"Well, since I haven't put him in a compromising position, I see no reason for this conversation," Kimberly said, rising from the chair to leave.

Laurie was on her feet as swiftly as a cat, the forgotten drink falling soundlessly to the carpeted deck.

"All right, keep your pretense of virtue. You'll find out the truth. And the truth is that what Chris Hawke wants is money. Money! He always wants more money. Money and his freedom, if he can get it. He loves me, but he won't marry me for that reason. He *will* marry me because my father has money."

Now it was Kimberly's turn to retaliate. Still retaining her cool, superior attitude, she tilted her head back, looked down her nose and said, "Then I feel very sorry for you." There was no tinge of pity in her voice, only scorn.

"You! You feel sorry for me?" Her blue eyes were blazing, her even white teeth gleaming in a grimace of hate. "Save your pity for yourself if you think Christopher Hawke is doing more than amusing himself with you."

127

Kimberly was already on the outer deck, but she turned, her lips curled in a cruel smile. "I'm sure your advice is good, Laurie, since you're obviously one of those dumb little girls who tried to compromise him, but, you see, I'm really not in a position to need it."

Kimberly hurried down the steps, not awaiting an answer, her hard-held anger too close to the surface, her outward calm too near to breaking. She forced herself to walk casually along the gravel drive, but her fists were clenched, her jaw clamped shut so tightly that her teeth hurt. But her anger was not the pure, blazing rage she would have preferred, for mixed with it was a tearing certainty that much of what Laurie had said about Hawke was true. He was unscrupulous, selfish, heartless, the kind of man she disliked on principle. But was it true that he would marry Laurie for her father's money?

Kimberly reached the marine store, praying that no one would be there. She needed time alone, time to compose herself. The room was blessedly empty, and she sank into the chair, staring unseeingly at the wall. As calmness gradually returned, and her splintered thoughts assumed some semblance of reason, she suddenly saw the entire episode for what it truly was: Laurie was jealous. She

128

was worried and unsure of herself. Even more to the point, she was unsure of Hawke. Best of all, Kimberly thought with elation, she thinks Hawke is interested in me. It was so blatantly obvious that Kimberly wondered why she had not known immediately. But then where Hawke was concerned, she always seemed to be involved in emotion more than reason. Suddenly a bubbling happiness rose in her at the idea that she could perhaps take Hawke away from Laurie. But would she even want to? There was something ruthless about him that frightened her. It was foolish, but even when he held her in his arms, there was fear mixed with the ecstasy she felt. *It's because I really don't like him*, she told herself. *I like nice men, men I can trust, men like Barry*. But liking had nothing to do with love, and even here, alone in the marine store, the memory of the night before brought a tingling excitement that Kimberly was helpless to combat. Her thoughts, warring with her feelings, brought on a restlessness that cried for activity; to escape her own confusion she hurried to the door, bent on finding something to occupy her. It would be impossible to sit here doing bookwork.

As she closed the door behind her she could see the long view down the driveway to the two yachts, and she stopped in surprise at the sight of Barry turning to wave to Laurie as he stepped ashore. Curiosity held her there, for she had not been aware that they had even met. Barry walked slowly, his hands in his pockets, his eyes staring down at his feet, the picture of a man deep in thought. He was on the steps leading up to the parking lot before he saw Kimberly, and there was no immediate look of pleasure at the encounter. He continued on doggedly, removing his hands from his pockets as he neared her. Kimberly's amber eyes narrowed in immediate suspicion. Had Laurie's vicious tongue been busy again?

Overriding that thought was the even more important news about the mortgage. Had Barry learned the worst? Was it Hawke who was trying to dispossess them? She waited as he neared, too fearful to go forward to meet him.

There was a worried look in his blue eyes and his face was creased in a frown. "I've been trying to call you, Kimberly," he said. "Where have you been?"

"I was taking a walk before I came here. Why, was it something important?"

"Well, yes, in a way."

"In a way? What do you mean? Tell me."

He hesitated for long moments, his frown deepening.

130

"Kimberly, let's go inside. I want to talk to you," he said with sudden decision.

She hurried inside, holding the door for him.

"Now what? What did you hear?" she demanded before he had even cleared the doorsill.

With maddening slowness he came in and carefully closed the door behind him.

"Kimberly, I know you're upset, but before we talk about it, I want to tell you the way I feel."

"The way you feel! Barry, in heaven's name just tell me what you heard."

"I want you to know I don't care." But his eyes looked miserable, seeming to say that he cared very much.

"Please just tell me."

"I'm telling you it doesn't matter." His voice was intense and quietly angry. Suddenly his hands were gripping her shoulders, his eyes narrowly searching her face as he looked down at her. Kimberly stared at him, reading the pain in his drawn face and intense expression.

"You know I've always loved you, and I want you to know that whatever happened on that island doesn't make any difference to me. Do you understand, Kimberly? I don't care."

131

She stared at him with wide, unbelieving eyes, too stunned for anger. Then his arms were around her, drawing her close.

"I can forgive you. I can't promise to forget, but I can forgive because I know it wasn't your fault. I know you, and I know that he must have taken advantage of the situation."

Her anger at Laurie had been superficial, because Laurie's insults had been self-serving, and the girl was a stranger, but this from Barry was a searing insult. All surprise dropped away in the rush of rage that swept her. He could forgive her! The words screamed in her mind, and she pushed violently away from him, her hands against his chest. But his arms held her.

"It's all right, Kimberly. I'm just trying to tell you that it's all right."

She could find no words to express the abuse she wanted to rain on him as a wave of disgust that verged on loathing washed over her. The thought that he could offer so magnanimously to forgive her in the same breath that he insulted her was infuriating. Well, she could never forgive him, but she was too choked with fury to speak.

"Am I interrupting something?"

There had been no warning sound of the door opening, and even Hawke's voice came to her dimly through the haze of her own violent anger. Her head turned toward him, her eyes wide but unseeing as the red mist that clouded her vision slowly dissipated.

Barry's arms dropped from her as he turned to face Hawke.

"If you don't mind, this is a private conversation," he said coolly.

"I can see that," Hawke told him casually, but the light of interest in his black eyes as he glanced from one to the other indicated that he had no intention of leaving until his curiosity was satisfied.

"Then, if you will, please leave."

Kimberly looked at Barry and wondered that she had never before noticed how pompous he was. There was no point in Hawke leaving, she thought, for she had no intention of making any explanations to Barry.

"He doesn't have to leave, Barry. We have nothing more to say."

Barry's glance came back to her, and a soft, pained expression replaced the coolness in his eyes. "We have," he said, "but we can talk about it later."

"We won't talk about it at all," Kimberly said, her voice rising. "Now please leave me alone."

He hesitated, obviously reluctant to leave her with Hawke.

"Just get out!" she cried, thinking that if she had to look at him another moment, she would claw his smug face.

Barry's shoulders slumped in defeat. "All right, Kimberly, but you do understand what I was trying to say?"

"Oh, I couldn't doubt what you were saying. You made it very clear." Her tone was acid, and Kimberly knew by Barry's slowly changing expression that he was beginning to doubt his own assumption of her guilt, but there was no forgiveness in her, only a vague wonder behind her anger, a wonder that she had never really known him at all, when she thought she had known him so well.

"We'll talk later," he said in a subdued voice. Kimberly's silence as she stared at him with angry eyes drove him toward the door, where he hesitated momentarily, his doubtful glance flitting from Kimberly to Hawke and back again to Kimberly before he closed the door behind him.

Hawke had been an interested spectator through it all, and now there was amusement in his face as he watched Kimberly.

"And I thought I had seen you in your worst tantrums," he finally said. "By the looks of you, he's lucky he got away without bodily injury."

134

Kimberly gave him a sour look, thinking he would probably yelp with laughter if she told him the reason for the argument.

"That friend of yours, Laurie, is a vicious cat," she could not resist saying, but trying at the same time to make it sound like a change of subject.

"Aha!" His eyes gleamed. "So that's it!"

"That's what?" Kimberly asked, immediately sorry she had spoken.

"She's been talking about us, and Mr. Barry Mead believes her lies."

Oh, she never should have let herself make that remark about Laurie; he was too sharp.

"Don't worry, Kimberly." There was reassurance in his tone, although his eyes still danced with amusement. "No one could possibly believe her; she's too obvious. Mead only believed her because he's in love with you, and that impairs his judgment."

The mention of love brought all her attention back to Hawke. Barry was forgotten as if he had never existed, as she looked up into Hawke's face. What he said was true, she thought; she loved him, and her emotions were forever getting in the way of her reason. As she looked into his copper-tan face, noting the arc of his winging brows and his tender, slightly amused black eyes, she wondered if he was as bad as she thought he was.

135

Her yearning always made her forget her doubts until something happened that made her swerve again to distrust and dislike.

"Don't look so tragic," he said, and his hand came up, the back of his knuckles gently brushing the side of her face. "If Mead thought the worse of you, he isn't worth your worry."

When he's like this, Kimberly thought, *I know I'm wrong. He couldn't be all the terrible things I think he is.*

His hand slipped beneath her hair, cupping her slender neck and drawing her toward him. Without volition, almost without thought, Kimberly went into his arms, surrendering to the sweet enchantment that enveloped her at his nearness. His dark head bent over her, his arm around her waist, arching her body close as their lips met. For Kimberly the moment was alive with meaning as a familiar delirium enveloped her.

She returned to the surrounding world with sharp dismay at the sound of voices and the loosening of Hawke's arms.

"Well!"

"Oh, my!"

Looking past Hawke, she saw Mrs. Kramer, her face puckered in dismay. Behind her Edna Turner, the worst gossip in Elsah, peered avidly over her shoulder, her

136

nose fairly twitching with eager curiosity.

"Come in, ladies," Hawke said easily.

It was obvious that he felt neither embarrassment nor resentment at their intrusion, but Kimberly knew that if her reputation was not already in shreds, it certainly would be now. Mrs. Kramer was an innocent gossip, but Edna Turner embroidered her spite with speculation. Although there was nothing wrong with Hawke's kissing her, this, combined with their night together on the island, could be built into a towering indictment against her, and would supply the town with gossip for months to come.

CHAPTER 10

Mr. Glass arrived in the last of the twilight, and although many of the customers were still aboard the Side Wheel, the boats were all moored, and Kimberly felt free to go home. It was already dark in the streets of Elsah and to Kimberly's dismay she saw no lights on in her own house. She went up the stairs, turning on lamps along the way, hoping Richard had merely gone to bed. But a depressed feeling, at one with the dismal evening, clung to her. Somehow she knew that she would not find him in the house. She stood in his doorway looking sadly into the empty room, knowing that there was only one thing that could have taken him from the house that night. So it was not over, as she had hoped; he was somewhere drinking, and she could only hope that it would not be followed by gambling.

The door knocker sounded and she turned, hurrying to answer it, but her steps slowed as she realized it could not be Richard.

Mrs. Kramer, her eyes round in her face, hurried in when Kimberly opened the door.

"Oh, Kimberly, I was watching for you to come home. Wasn't it terrible that Edna Turner saw you with that man Hawke?"

"It wasn't terrible at all," Kimberly said, trying to keep the annoyance from her voice. Mrs. Kramer obviously relished this kind of conversation and was as eager as a teen-ager to indulge in girlish chatter. "We're both adults, and a kiss doesn't exactly indicate a loss of virtue."

"Oh, no, I didn't mean it did, but I've been wanting to tell you about that Benning girl. She saw that notice you put in the store and had me over to clean her boat this morning. And, Kimberly, she asked all kinds of questions about you. I didn't think anything about it, but then after we talked awhile, she started saying things about you. You know, about you being on that island with him and coming back with some of your clothes off."

Kimberly sighed, closing her eyes with weariness while she wondered what innocent gossip Mrs. Kramer had divulged that, in Laurie's hands, could be twisted into something damning. Whatever it was, she was certain that Barry had been the recipient of some of it – not that she cared about Barry.

"Mrs. Kramer, I don't care what Laurie Benning is saying about me" – which was not entirely true – "and everyone knows that Edna Turner is a vicious gossip."

"Yes, but you know everyone will say, 'Where there's smoke there's fire,' and a young girl can't be too careful of her reputation."

"Well, what do you want me to do about it?"

They were still standing in the foyer, and Kimberly knew she should ask Mrs. Kramer to sit down or have a cup of coffee, but she felt emotionally drained. The woman's very eagerness was an affront.

"I don't know what you can do, but I thought you should know," Mrs. Kramer said uncertainly.

139

"Well, thank you for letting me know, but I don't think my knowing will stop either Laurie Benning or Edna Turner."

The conversation dragged on desultorily until Mrs. Kramer, obviously disappointed that Kimberly had neither risen to the challenge of the situation nor indulged in girlish reminiscences about her night on the island, reluctantly made her departure.

Kimberly wandered back to the kitchen, realizing that part of her exhaustion was caused by hunger, and hoped there was something to eat. She had to settle for bacon, eggs, and toast, and while she ate, her mind went back over the day, her thoughts lingering longest on the times she had been with Hawke. She ate automatically, hardly aware of the food, her eyes passing over the softly lighted kitchen but seeing nothing. Forgetting that she disliked and distrusted Hawke, she recalled only the light in his dark eyes when he looked at her and the breathless happiness that flooded her when she was near him and let herself forget all her doubts about him. And Laurie was jealous, so jealous, she was desperate. Did she have good reason to be jealous? Kimberly wondered suddenly. Then slowly, like the opening of a flower, the thought blossomed in Kimberly's mind: Why shouldn't she have him if she wanted him? She had done nothing but fight against loving him, fight against liking him. Even after she knew she loved him, she had fought against her feelings, not trusting herself any more than she did him. Well, that's in the past, she decided; in the future things will be different. Exactly what she would do she did not know, but she confidently assured herself that she *would* know when the time came. And then she realized that her love for Hawke would solve all her other problems. With Hawke as her husband the marina would be saved for Richard.

The sound of the door knocker interrupted her happy musings, and Kimberly went through the hall, hoping that Mrs. Kramer had not returned. But it was Hawke who stood on the porch, as if conjured up by her own thoughts.

"Come in," she told him, hearing the breathless note in her voice.

He looked at her alertly before saying, "I came to see your father. Is he home?"

He was already stepping into the entrance hall as Kimberly said, "No, he isn't, but I can help you, if it's something about business."

"If you recall, I wanted to see his books."

"Oh." Kimberly felt breathless, all the confidence she had had while eating her eggs and making her plans having drained away.

She wanted to keep him here, but didn't know how to accomplish this without being too obvious; she had never before planned purposely to maneuver a man.

"Is anything wrong?" Hawke asked sharply, peering again into her face.

"No. No, I was just thinking that the books are at the marina. I keep them there. Would you care for a drink?"

"Sounds like a good idea. Will your father be home soon?"

"I don't know," she told him as she led the way into the parlor, where they kept a small bar in an old pine cabinet.

Kimberly switched on a table lamp and then took bottles and glasses from the cabinet.

"I like this room," Hawke said as he sank appreciatively onto the couch. "Is this a real Oriental rug?"

"I think so. It's quite old. I'll have to go to the kitchen for some ice."

When she returned with the ice bucket, she smiled with relief, for although it was not cold, Hawke had started a small fire in the fireplace and was feeding it twigs to encourage the logs to catch. Surely a man who lighted a fire was preparing to stay for a while. He rose with the litheness Kimberly had noticed when she first saw him, and came to stand behind her shoulder as she finished mixing the drinks. Then, as he took his drink, his hand closed over hers, and he led her to the couch facing the fireplace.

They sat quietly staring into the mounting flames, her hand, still nestled in his, resting on the couch between them. When the logs caught and flared high, Hawke put his drink on the table and switched off the lamp, leaving the room lighted only by the dancing glow of the fire.

It was a romantic setting, Kimberly thought, thankful that Hawke had created it himself for it would have been too obvious if she had been the one to light the fire and switch off the lamp. She watched him covertly, flicking little glances at him from the corner of her eye. He appeared perfectly relaxed and content, occasionally sipping his drink, his gaze on the flickering flames that reflected off his black eyes, giving them a liquid quality. Kimberly was tinglingly aware of her hand in his warm one, her shoulder brushing his. In nervous haste she almost gulped her drink and then wondered if she should have another. She felt a tension mounting that made it impossible for her to relax drowsily and enjoy this quiet firelit peace.

"There's something about this house,"

Hawke said. "I don't know what it is, but it seems to cast a spell. It gives me the feeling that there's no hurry about anything, that everything is as it should be, and all you have to do is sit back and let it happen."

"Mmm," Kimberly murmured in agreement, not wanting to break the spell.

Then he turned and looked down at her, his eyes moving over her face intently as if studying each feature. When their eyes met and held, Kimberly felt consumed by his dark, hot gaze. Slowly he leaned toward her and, when his lips touched hers, her breath came in a soft, short gasp, willing him to take her in his arms. But after that one kiss he merely released her hand and put his arm around her, drawing her head to his shoulder and again leaning back in contemplation of the fire.

"Tell me about this Barry Mead," he said after a long silence.

"There's nothing to tell about him," Kimberly said, resenting his bringing Barry into the conversation when she wanted him to be thinking only of her.

"There must be something. I thought I had seen you angry, but you were on the thin edge of control when I came into the marine store."

144

"It was nothing, and I don't want to talk about him." And then, feeling that what she had said made it seem more important than it was, she added, "It's just that I thought we were friends, and he said something that made me know we could never be friends."

"So he believes the gossip."

Kimberly lifted her head to stare at him questioningly.

"Oh, yes, I've been hearing it too," he said.

"From Laurie?" she asked.

One eyebrow cocked high on his forehead. "Have you been talking to Laurie?"

"It's more like she's been talking to me." Now Kimberly welcomed the conversation, hoping she could learn his exact relationship to Laurie, who claimed he loved her.

"That should have been an interesting conversation." His eyes were dancing with amusement. "I wish I had been there. I'm certain you didn't take Laurie's brand of spite meekly. Tell me, which one of you would you say won?"

Her head came up from his shoulder, and she stared angrily into his face. "I don't bandy words with people like Laurie," she told him angrily.

He smiled complacently. "Then I should be flattered. You do bandy words with me. In

145

fact, it seems that you take every occasion to do so."

She frowned at him, and then a smile crept into her face. "You're just maddening, and that makes a difference."

"And you're different from any girl I've ever known."

That surprised Kimberly, for she thought of herself as very average, but she would never admit this to Hawke. All her hopes depended on his thinking her someone very rare and special.

Then his hands were on her shoulders, turning her so that he cradled her across his lap, his arms supporting her shoulders, his other hand at her waist. His dark face hovered above her for a moment, and Kimberly could see an eager light deep in his eyes that was more than the reflection of the fire. And then he was drawing her to him, one hand against the small of her back as he lifted her shoulders. His lips met hers in a long, deep kiss as Kimberly clung to him, an arm about his neck, holding him close. All the wild ecstasy she had known before when he held her in his arms was with her again, only now there was no retreating, no drawing away in surprised shock at her own surging emotions. His lips moved from her mouth to her throat as he drew her to him in a hard embrace.

146

Kimberly's breath came in short, sharp pants against the straight column of his neck. He held her quietly against him for a long time, and Kimberly noted with keen pleasure that his chest heaved with his own disrupted breathing. *He loved her*, her happy heart sang, and in a moment he would tell her so. She had won, and it had all been so simple. All she had had to do was stop fighting and let herself love him.

Through her soaring happiness she suddenly became aware that he was very silent, almost as if he was waiting for something. She lifted her head from his shoulder, her lips trailing across his cheek seeking his mouth, but suddenly his hands were gripping her shoulders, dragging her clinging arms away from him. With a swiftness that startled Kimberly he lifted her in his arms as he arose, turned, and put her down on the couch. Sitting beside her, his hands braced on either side of her, he glowered down into her face.

"Do you recall what I told you, Kimberly?" Although his voice was soft, there was suppressed rage in it, and even in the dimness of the firelight she could read the anger in his face. But confusion at this sudden metamorphosis held her speechless; she could not think how to

147

answer his question, for she had no idea what he meant.

"Do you remember?" His hands were on her shoulders in a hard grip, almost shaking her.

"I don't know what you mean," she finally cried, her eyes searching his face for an explanation of his sudden anger.

"Why are you doing this?" he demanded.

She stared mutely back at him; it was impossible to look into that furious face and say she loved him. He had said nothing of love.

"I told you it was dangerous to try to use me," he said. "Didn't you believe me?"

The memory of that night on the island and his terrible anger came back to her. With a sinking heart she realized that he thought tonight was no more than a trick to try to save the marina for her father. Resentment that he should tarnish this magic evening with his hateful suspicions rose in her and quickly turned to anger.

"What did you expect?" she said, lashing out at him, but even beneath her rising anger was the hope that he would say he loved her and expected her to love him.

"Actually I guess I should have been suspicious as soon as I walked in. I knew you were different. There was something about

148

you that was less untouchable. And then there was the fire all nicely made and the offer of a drink."

"You lighted the fire."

"As I was, no doubt, intended to do. If you had met me in anything but those slacks and blouse, I would have been alerted immediately."

"You are suspicious and hateful."

"And you're a complete failure as a femme fatale." He smiled a cruel, wicked smile. "But that's no reason why we should call a halt to this interesting scene, is it?"

His hand was suddenly at the neckline of her blouse, loosening the buttons. In outraged modesty Kimberly slapped him with one hand as she struggled to rise, but he leaned toward her, forcing her back.

"You don't like to play the game if you're not in control?" he asked, his face only inches away from hers.

The unexplained fear that he could rouse in her came back with force. She had thought it was sparked only by her own emotional turmoil, but now she realized how little she actually knew Hawke.

"Get away from me," she said, forcing her voice to sound calm, determined not to let him see her fear any more than she would let him know she loved him.

149

"All in good time," he said as his lips closed on hers in a hard, bruising kiss.

Kimberly remained rigid, resenting his roughness, refusing to respond except for the pressure of her hands against his chest trying to force him away. Then his lips softened, became caressing. One hand slipped beneath her shoulders, lifting her to him, and the other curved around the nape of her neck, moving sensuously around to her throat and then brushing the already partially opened blouse aside to bare her shoulder.

Kimberly hung in a limbo of uncertainty, no longer fighting against him but unable to resist his skilled lovemaking. Her heart fluttered madly at the feel of his warm breath against her bare skin as his lips moved on her shoulder. It was as if the terrible scene moments before had never happened. A shred of cautious doubt remained but, despite that uncertainty, her arms moved to encircle him, to hold him closer as her mind rocked with contradictory emotions. When his lips moved to hers again, she returned his kiss, letting the doubts drift away as if they had never existed. But in a moment he released her so suddenly that her head fell back against the couch cushion, and he was again looking down into her face, a slow smile on his lips that never reached his eyes.

"How far are you willing to go to save that marina?" he asked with suave brutality, and her amber eyes flew wide open in shocked dismay.

His black eyes raked her face, seeming to study her with clinical interest, but there was no softness in his expression, rather a restrained anger that showed in the grim narrowing of his lips.

Kimberly was sputtering with rage as she tried to sit up, her doubled fists beating on him while tears burned behind her eyes. She bit her lip with a determination that he would not see her cry.

"You're loathsome," she finally gasped. "Get away. Let me go."

He rose as if it was a matter of complete indifference to him, and she scrambled to her feet. The realization that he had purposely tried to arouse her passion and succeeded was like burning gall, making her feel almost sick, and the lump in her throat, which threatened to dissolve any moment into tears, held her silent as she glared at him through narrowed lids. At the moment she hated him, only wanted him out of her sight and out of the house so that she could release the iron control required even to stand there looking at him.

"One thing I do have to admire is your
151

determination and loyalty. Your father is a lucky man."

"Get out," she whispered through clenched teeth.

"All right, I'll get out. But aren't you going to tell me first about your being an incurable romantic?"

She threw herself at him with doubled fists, no longer caring about self-control, but he dodged easily, and moved toward the door. As it closed behind him Kimberly sank weakly against the panels, tears raining down her face and filling her throat so that she sobbed in a way she had not done since she was a small child.

CHAPTER 11

The night seemed endless as Kimberly tossed in her bed, reliving each facet of the evening. When her tears had finally stopped, she felt drained and hollow, too numb to retain the fury that had driven her to strike out at Hawke. Over and over again she asked herself how he could have so misjudged her. And why, oh, why, she asked herself, as she plumped her limp pillow, was he so quick to assume she could not love him? Surely she was not the first one. Or did he mistrust all women? With that thought Kimberly immediately resented being classified with other women. She should hate him, she knew. He had been brutal, obnoxious, and intentionally insulting. Perhaps some woman in the past had caused him to be like this. The idea made her immediately jealous of that woman, whoever she might be. But then an even worse thought bloomed in her mind. Perhaps he just did not want her love. Laurie had said he wanted to be free.

Sometime during the night she heard Richard come home. After a fleeting prayer of thankfulness for his return and a hope that he had not lost more money gambling, her thoughts returned to the painful evening that had started so beautifully.

Although there was no sign of dawn at the windows, the birds were chirping hesitantly, as if still half asleep, when Kimberly dragged herself from bed. She was weary and hollow-eyed, having tossed most of the night but no longer able to endure her circling and repetitious thoughts.

Through careful application of the makeup she seldom wore, Kimberly looked better than she felt when she arrived at the marina.

There was a crisp freshness to her white slacks and blue-and-white striped T-shirt. Her brown hair was brushed to a deep sheen and held back from her face with a broad white band. Only the weariness in her eyes betrayed her sleepless night.

The sun was low in the clear blue sky, painting gold on the ripples of the water, and there was that special early-morning freshness to the clean air that was like a delicate perfume. The soft breeze coming off the water held the smell of the river, more provocative now in the early-morning hours than later, when the sun was high. The marina was deserted – not even Mr. Glass was in evidence – and Kimberly stood at the top of the steps leading down from the parking lot and gazed about her. The wide expanse of water; the gently bobbing boats; the tree-shrouded islands; the headlands jutting out into the river; the line of towering bluffs, white and gold in the sunlight; and the seemingly endless blue sky – it was all so much a part of her life that she had never realized what it meant to her until now, when she was about to lose it. She loved them. The marina was part of Richard's life too, although he had lost sight of that now. Suddenly she knew that it was not just the security for the future that the marina offered, but a way of life that she was fighting desperately to save for Richard – and for herself too.

Yet Hawke would take it all away from them, she suddenly thought, and once again she was back on the treadmill of the night before. Shaking herself to cast off unwelcome thoughts, Kimberly went down the steps. She would check the boat she had started to paint and Jimmy had later finished. If he had done a good enough job, perhaps she could make painting a part of his general work. With stubborn determination she focused on the work to be done, brushing from her mind the knowledge that before long she might no longer be making these decisions.

She walked down the road, her canvas shoes making rasping sounds on the gravel, watching her shadow moving before her but acutely aware of Hawke's cruiser just ahead. She was grateful that it was too early for anyone to be about. She had no wish to face him again so soon. How would he act when they did meet again?

She was passing the Bennings' yacht when a gay, girlish voice called, "Hello, there. You're up early."

Kimberly looked up to see Laurie standing at the rail, her diaphanous peignoir rippling in the slight breeze. A movement beyond her caught Kimberly's eye, and she stared

155

in open-mouthed surprise as Hawke came out of the cabin. When he saw her on the driveway, his brows rushed together in a black frown, but Laurie's lips were curved in a smug, triumphant smile.

At first there was only surprise as the details of this early-morning tableau tumbled into place, stating more explicitly than words that Hawke had spent the night with Laurie. Then came a feeling of betrayal, and then resentment as sharp as if Hawke were her own husband caught with another woman. How could he do this? her mind cried. How could he leave me and go to that tramp?

"Laurie, go inside and get dressed."

His voice was harsh, and as Laurie turned to speak she seemed to hesitate; then without a word or a glance at Kimberly she moved toward the cabin door.

Hawke took her place at the rail, gazing down at Kimberly with a slightly mocking smile and one eyebrow cocked questioningly, as if waiting to hear what she would say. But she was without words. There was only a numb pain in her heart and a feeling of desolation. Her startled eyes were on him, and then, biting her lip to keep it from trembling, she ducked her head and hurried toward the paint shack.

She was unaware that he had followed until

he walked into the building. She turned, feeling almost at bay, wanting nothing other than to run away, but pride kept her staring defiantly up at him.

"Kimberly, what kind of an innocent are you?" he asked, his black eyes searching her face, holding her gaze despite her wish to turn away.

"I don't want to talk about your affairs," she told him.

"I don't want to talk about my affairs either. I want to talk about you."

"After the way you acted last night, you should be aware that I don't want to talk to you about anything, least of all about me. Now please go away and leave me alone." Her head was high and there was a flash of anger in her eyes, but inside she was torn by conflicting emotions. During the entire sleepless night she had tried to resolve her feelings, but her efforts had come to nothing. Now this flaunting of his affair with Laurie seemed to leave her helpless. She could only show disapproval, for never, never could she let him know how much it hurt her.

He had been studying her thoughtfully. "You deserved that last night," he said. "If you had come out honestly and asked me not to buy the marina, there could have been some basis for agreement, but no, you had to play this game to get what you wanted without having to ask."

She would choke on the truth, she thought, before she would tell him it had been no game. It was no longer just a matter of pride, for she felt, somehow, that if he ever knew she loved him, she would be at his mercy. She had no idea what he might do, and she had no wish to learn.

"Could we have come to some agreement?" she finally asked.

"I guess that would have depended on what you wanted."

"What I want is the marina. I don't want you to take over that mortgage and leave us with practically nothing." There, it was said; and if he was the one who had been inquiring about it at the bank, she would soon know.

"Why are you so determined to keep this place? It's an albatross around your neck. Your father spends the money faster than you can make it."

"What my father does is none of your business," she told him angrily, hating to have to defend Richard this way.

"It's as if you're expecting me to pass up a good business deal for his sake." There was no resentment in his tone because of her angry words; he was merely telling her.

"You don't care about anyone. You're
158

selfish and cruel and can't understand doing something for someone just out of consideration." Kimberly knew this was useless, but as long as there was a shred of hope that he might let them keep the marina, she had to try.

"If you mean financing the marina so your father can gamble away the profits, no, I'm not fool enough to do that."

She opened her mouth to answer him but he was still speaking, not waiting for an answer. "About last night –"

"I don't want to talk about last night," she said, turning to leave.

"I just thought I'd let you know that I enjoyed it as much as you did."

She swung toward him, wanting to scorch him with hot words, but it would be useless to deny her enjoyment and would only prolong this unwelcome conversation. Making a sound of exasperation, she stared at him with stormy eyes, then turned and fled down the gravel road toward the point of land along the outer edge of the marina, at the end of which the Side Wheel was moored.

Eager to get away from the house and her own thoughts, Kimberly had had no breakfast, and as she often did, had planned to eat at the Side Wheel, hoping it was too early for Barry to be there. At the thought of

159

Barry she recalled her angry hurt at him the day before. That argument not only seemed trivial and unimportant now but far in the past. Strange to think it was only yesterday. So much had happened since then.

As she made coffee in the huge kitchen Kimberly tried to keep her thoughts away from Hawke. Her appetite was gone now, and she paced the deck, waiting for the coffee to perk, gazing with unseeing eyes out the wide windows at the expanse of river as she tried to fight off the depression that hung over her. There was no glimmer of hope anywhere. She would lose the marina. Already her high hopes for Richard had been crushed by his disappearance the night before. Certainly Barry would sell the Side Wheel now, and Hawke preferred Laurie's free and easy morals to her love.

The door opened and Barry stood hesitantly, his hand on the knob, studying her.

"Kimberly –" he finally said into the silence.

"Hello, Barry." Suddenly she was happy to see him, relieved to have someone to talk to. Her anger of the day before seemed unimportant now.

"Kimberly." He hurried toward her, his hand outstretched, a worried look on his lean face. "I should never have said what I did. I know you. I know it wasn't true."

"It's all right, Barry. Will you have some coffee?"

"It isn't all right. It was unforgivable. I can only – Kimberly, I was jealous. I was out of my mind, and then –"

"And then you talked with Laurie," she finished for him with a faint smile on her lips.

"She really didn't say much. If she had, I would have defended you. But she implied – I don't know how she did it but I just knew – well, I knew what she believed. When I saw you with him the night before – Well, everything seemed to fit in with what I was feeling and I didn't even stop to think."

"I didn't know she could be that clever. But you don't have to explain, Barry. I understand."

For the first time she did understand. Seeing Hawke and Laurie together this morning had given her the same sick feeling she knew Barry must have felt when he thought she had been like that with Hawke. Now she felt a sad tenderness for him.

Kimberly poured coffee, and they sat at one of the small tables where the staff ate. Through the window beside them the sun, reflecting off the water, threw moving lights into the room that danced along the table and across their faces as they sat opposite each other.

As he spooned sugar into his coffee Barry smiled at her for the first time since he had come into the room. "I didn't really expect to be forgiven," he told her. Having him there was easing some of the depressing loneliness Kimberly had been feeling, and she smiled back at him, thinking they were a miserable pair; he, in love with her, she, loving Hawke, and Hawke – Well, Hawke was with Laurie.

"I've been thinking," Barry said. "I'm not going to sell the Side Wheel to Hawke."

"But you said it was losing money!"

"It is, but keeping it isn't going to break me. After he's gone, I'll close it and later look for another buyer."

"Barry, I don't want you to do that for us. It might not do any good, anyway. Last night Dad was gone when I came home. He didn't come in until sometime this morning. If he can't take over some of the work and keeps gambling, we'll lose the marina anyway."

"But you don't want that."

"You know I don't. It's just that I'll have no choice. I'm keeping the money we're making, but if he owes those gamblers, he'll have to pay them eventually, and there won't be anything I can do but give him whatever I have. You see, you might be sacrificing a

162

chance to sell without helping us at all."

"Just because Richard went to town doesn't mean he isn't going to try to work the marina. Do you know he was gambling?"

"No, but he always has."

"Well, then let's just wait and see. Hawke wants the Side Wheel as part of the marina. If he can't have it, he might change his mind and not even try to get the marina. I hate to have to tell you, but I saw Mike last night, and it *was* Hawke who was inquiring at the bank about the mortgage."

Although it was no surprise to Kimberly, she felt an unexpected stab of pain and disappointment. Her mind fled back to the night before when Hawke had held her in his arms, his lips gentle on hers. All the time he had been planning this. The stark perfidy of it should have made her hate him more, but she could only feel a dismal ache of loss for something that she knew she had never really had.

Kimberly was unaware that her thoughts were clearly readable in her wide, tragic eyes until Barry said in a soft, husky voice, "You're in love with him, aren't you, Kimberly?"

"How can you think that?" she asked bitterly.

"I think I must have known it when you came back from that island. I think that's why it wasn't hard for Laurie to make me think what I did."

There was a pained look in his eyes as he studied her face, and finally, when she said nothing, her eyes on the coffee she was slowly stirring in her cup, he asked, "Kimberly, did he say something last night to make you think he wouldn't take the marina?"

Her brows flew together in a frown as her eyes met his, with the beginning of anger in them. "How did you know I saw him last night?"

"I came by your house to talk to you. When I saw his car there, I didn't come in. You just told me Richard wasn't home, so Hawke must have been there to see you."

Slightly mollified, she told him, "He came to see Dad, but he wasn't home. And he didn't tell me what he wanted." Then another thought occurred to her. "Barry, could they take the marina away from us without even telling us about it?"

Barry was reluctant to answer but finally he said, "I'm afraid they can. But that doesn't mean you can't find out about it beforehand," he added quickly. "I can check the legal publications. If there's going to be a foreclosure sale, it will be in one of them."

"Will that do us any good?"

"I'm afraid not, unless you can pay off what

164

you owe. All it will do is let you know you're being foreclosed."

The employees who worked aboard the Side Wheel were beginning to arrive, for it was Sunday and the restaurant would be open. No longer able to continue a private conversation Kimberly and Barry left the Side Wheel. Although Kimberly had walked the long way around to reach the boat, Barry had used her outboard, so they came out on the harbor side of the old boat. Kimberly's eyes almost immediately flew to the far end of the marina where the yachts were moored, but now only the Bennings' yacht was there.

Noting her glance, Barry said, "They were gassing up when I came over. Didn't you see them going up the river?"

"No. I didn't notice. I was just surprised to see the cruiser gone. I didn't know they were going out."

Kimberly had heard the anger in Hawke's voice when he told Laurie to get dressed, but obviously it had meant little.

Well, she would forget them, she told herself, not think about Hawke at all. But for the rest of the day she was keenly alert to every boat moving on the river, waiting, despite herself, for Hawke's return. As the day darkened into evening she wondered if he would ever return.

CHAPTER 12

During the following week Kimberly saw little of Hawke, although she was constantly aware of his comings and goings. To her aching dismay he was usually with Laurie, and they were often gone on daylong excursions. At these times she waited with little patience, fearful that he would leave for good without a word of good-bye. A check to pay for his rental of the mooring, or a notice that he had bought the marina would be the last word she would hear from him. At other times she wondered what kept him here, for certainly his business with Richard or the bank could not be drawn out this long.

She had refrained from telling Richard that Hawke was inquiring about the mortgage, but occasionally she questioned him, hoping to learn what business was holding Hawke at Cartwright's Landing. It soon became obvious that Richard was as perplexed as she was.

"I don't know if he's lost interest in the marina or is just making me wait and hoping for a better price," Richard mused. "Has he said anything to you about it, Kitten?"

"No, he hasn't," Kimberly told him, not

admitting that she had seen him only at a distance during the past week.

By the end of the week she had decided that he was purposely avoiding her. There could be but one reason for this; he was buying the mortgage and would soon foreclose on them. Yet she found it difficult to believe that Hawke would ever feel ashamed of what he did. It seemed far more in character for him to claim brazenly that any man who could not take care of his business deserved to lose it, and insist that she see the reasonableness of his attitude.

Despite her suspicions, her anger at his frequent absences, and her resentment at being ignored, Kimberly could not dispel the ache in her heart nor control the leaping excitement that rose in her at the sight of him on the dock or in the parking lot.

The week had been exceptionally busy, so busy that she had little time, except during the short evenings, to brood. The marina was crowded every day with people taking early vacations, and they swarmed about the docks from early morning until late dusk. Most of Kimberly's paperwork was neglected as she spent her time with customers who claimed her attention, either demanding work on their boats or merely being sociable. In addition there were long-time customers who missed

167

the convenience of the Side Wheel and often asked her to open it for a few hours. Since most of her time was spent with people, Kimberly found it convenient to see them there instead of in the marine store, but it did mean extra work. Barry had the boat cleaned each Monday, and Kimberly, in all conscience, felt she had to leave it as clean at the end of each day as she had found it. This meant vacuuming, wiping tables, and cleaning up the used cups and glasses in the evening before she went home. Yet she was willing to do this, assuring herself that after the regatta this coming Saturday, there would be less inclination on the part of the boaters to gather together for conversation, most of which was about the coming race. All the sailboat owners were in a state of happy anticipation, promising to beat each other and even making bets among themselves about the outcome.

Thus, despite her uncertainty and anxious yearning over Hawke, Kimberly was kept too busy to brood about it. Yet at night, weary though she was from the long day, sleep often eluded her. Memories of Hawke, his arms around her, his lips against hers, stirred her to an aching longing. She lived over and over again the times they had been together, until loneliness for him welled up in her; tears rose at the memory of his casual wave or nod when he saw her now. Then anger at herself would replace her useless daydreaming, and anger at Hawke, too, when she thought of the marina. Finally, in utter exhaustion, she would fall into a deep, almost drugged, sleep.

Saturday arrived and with it the crowds who would participate in the regatta. Kimberly was at the marina early, but already there were many people moving about the docks, some making last-minute checks on their boats, others visiting in scattered groups. She stood on the graveled road near the foot of the steps, gazing at the colorful scene. They were a well-dressed crowd in their smart sport clothes, the brilliant colors flashing in the sunlight, and there was a happy air of excitement that erupted in the trilling laughter of the women and the deeper voices of the men calling to each other from dock to dock. The day was sparkling with sunshine, the blue of the sky reflected in the water like a backdrop for the entire marina. A breeze, milky warm and not too brisk, moved down the river, eliciting approving remarks from the contestants. Unattached young men wandered along the docks, stopping here and there to talk with girls who welcomed their attentions. Other young people separated from family groups in search of their contemporaries.

"How do you like that?" a tall man standing near Kimberly remarked to anyone who would listen. "My daughter is sailing with Phil Bailey. And she's the best sailor on the river!"

Kimberly smiled, not at all surprised that Phil had garnered the best for himself. She knew the girl, who was not only a good sailor but also very attractive.

The man wandered off, and Kimberly moved along the gravel drive, stopping here and there at different docks to talk with the people she knew best and to greet those who were newcomers to Cartwright's Landing. All the regulars were there: the Coreys with their friend Martha Lansing, who had been impressed by the Side Wheel salon; Julie and Craig Dutton and their friends the Caswells, who were not participating in the regatta but had rented a boat to pace the racers; and Phil Bailey, with several friends and the girl he had lured away from her father. Kimberly greeted them all, but as she visited with them her eyes wandered, looking around and past the crowds for a glimpse of Hawke. Both he and Laurie had signed the list for the dinner dance, and she half expected them to be there for the regatta too, although neither was participating. But the *Pandora* was still at its mooring, and Kimberly had not seen either of them, nor had they joined the people on the docks.

As the time for the start of the race neared, several boats began moving out onto the river, and Kimberly turned to Martha Lansing, who appeared to be alone now that the Coreys had boarded their boat.

"Come over to the Side Wheel to watch the race," she said. "Everyone who isn't on the river will be there. You can see all the way up the river from the foredeck, or watch from the bar. It's in the forepart of the boat too."

"I'd like that," Martha said with mounting enthusiasm. "I didn't know there was a bar."

"We might as well go over now. It looks like everyone is ready," Kimberly told her and led the way to her own boat.

Those in cruisers and motorboats, who would watch the regatta from the water, were already underway, moving toward the small island far upstream where the sailors would turn, rounding the island for their return trip.

Kimberly left Martha on the Side Wheel, walked around the deck to the far side, and stepped ashore again on the narrow strip of land that formed the outer perimeter of the harbor, where she waited for the contestants to form a line, sails still furled. When they

171

were ready, she lowered the flag that signaled the start of the race. The white sails flapped out, catching the breeze, and were quickly hoisted until they formed a line of bright white triangles against the blue of the water and green of the islands beyond.

Despite the perfection of the day, and the enthusiasm and gay camaraderie of the spectators, Kimberly felt little pleasure in the affair, and as she reboarded the Side Wheel to join the others, she felt weary of the holiday spirits that buoyed the others. She wanted to be far away from them, where she could worry and brood and not be forced to respond to their gay banter and idle chatter.

Some of the people were in the salon, but most were gathered in the bar, where the curving line of windows at the front of the boat presented a panoramic view of the river looking upstream. Although some people were clustered at the windows to watch the race, less avid fans were leaning on the bar, glass in hand, or seated at the small tables in pairs and groups. Kimberly saw Martha Lansing at one of the tables with a man who looked vaguely familiar. At the same time Martha saw her and waved to her to join them. As she sat down Martha introduced the man, and Kimberly acknowledged the introduction, immediately forgetting his name as she saw Hawke and Laurie come through the doorway.

Following her glance, Martha turned her head and in a voice ringing with delight, called, "Laurie!"

The sulky expression on Laurie's face changed to a smile as she recognized Martha. Her blue eyes lighted with pleasure as she moved toward the table, seemingly unaware of Kimberly or the man with them.

"What are you doing here?" Martha asked at the same time that Laurie was saying, "I didn't know you lived near here."

"Sit down." Martha indicated a chair that Hawke held as Laurie seated herself, but Kimberly had eyes only for Hawke, who smiled and nodded to her over Laurie's blond head.

It was the first time Kimberly had been this close to him in a week, and she felt a weak hollowness somewhere beneath her breastbone as she looked into his tanned face. But when their eyes met, his were cool and indifferent, as if she were a stranger in whom he had little interest.

Martha and Laurie interrupted their eager conversation long enough to make introductions as Hawke sat down next to Laurie.

"You'll have to excuse us," Martha said. "We went to school together. We were roommates and it's been ... How long has it been, Laurie?"

"I don't know, but whatever it is, it's too long. Tell me, what have you been doing? Are you married?"

Kimberly stopped listening. She was not only uninterested, but felt the conversation excluded the others at the table, leaving them to make their own small talk. Kimberly was silent, all her attention centered on Hawke, who was equally silent. The other man – Kimberly had again missed his name in the introductions – asked a few questions of Hawke: Did he have a boat at the marina? What kind was it? Did he come from this area? Hawke answered the questions politely but did so little to encourage the conversation that the man finally fell silent.

"You've had a busy week," Hawke finally said to Kimberly; his eyes were on the people crowding the small bar.

"Yes," she answered, feeling strained and ill at ease. "It's always like this at regatta time." There were so many other things she wanted to say to him, but not here, not now with the others listening. Some things she wanted to say could never be said, like, Why have you avoided me? Did you buy the mortgage? and Do you really love Laurie? But most of all she wanted to see his eyes light up

174

when he looked at her, and to feel his arms around her again. Oh, to be again in his arms and able to forget all her fears, to ease the terrible yearnings that seemed to fill her every idle moment.

"Are you coming to the dance tonight?" she asked, knowing that he was, but feeling she had to attempt some conversation.

"Yes." He was still watching the others at the bar, and when he said nothing more, Kimberly turned to the other man, a feeling of desperation filling her. "And you, Mr. –"

"Steed. Luke Steed." His smile was friendly, but his eyes held a watchfulness as he glanced from her to Hawke and back again, as if he felt the tension between them and knew its cause.

"Are you coming to the dance?" Kimberly asked, feeling her face flush at the knowing look in his shrewd eyes.

"I'm a guest here, and I don't know if I qualify."

"If you're a guest of one of our people, you're welcome," Kimberly told him.

"Then I'll be here. I think I might become one of your people. I like this." He nodded to indicate the bar, the salon, and the gathering in general.

At that moment a ripple of comment came from those gathered at the window, catching

175

Steed's attention. "If you'll excuse me, I think I'll see what's going on."

Kimberly nodded, and he left the table. She knew what was happening. One of the boaters had probably put forth a burst of speed and was drawing swiftly away from the others. She was relieved the man had gone; his knowing glance had made her uncomfortable, and now she could turn her full attention to Hawke, for Laurie and Martha were still reminiscing about school days.

"I haven't seen you much lately," she said, hoping to prod him into an explanation of his reasons for avoiding her.

His eyes came back to hers, still cool and distant. "I've been busy."

"And what keeps you so busy?" she asked, not caring if she was prying.

He smiled slightly. "You *are* inquisitive today, aren't you?"

Anger flared in Kimberly, but before she could answer, Laurie turned, her hair swinging with the swiftness of her movement. It was apparent that she had not been as engrossed in her conversation as she had appeared, for her glance stabbed at Kimberly as she put a possessive hand on Hawke's arm and then smiled up into his face.

"Martha and I were the most popular girls in our class," she told him. "You might call

176

us rivals; we were always taking boys away from each other."

"So you're not so much friends as old enemies," Hawke said.

"We are friends," Laurie pouted. "Men just can't understand."

"I understand. You're like old soldiers. You like to reminisce about battles past. And with you, my sweet, the war is never really over."

Kimberly listened in wonder at the barely disguised rudeness in the languor of Hawke's remarks. It was almost, she thought, as if he was tired of listening to Laurie, annoyed with her self-serving remarks about her popularity, and restless, too, at her constant possessiveness that was epitomized now by the hand clutching his arm. But even as she thought this Kimberly was aware that he made no attempt to draw away from her.

A murmur of dismay came from those at the window, and one voice clear above the muted comments asked, "Did the boat capsize?"

Kimberly was on her feet, moving between the crowded onlookers, fearful of an accident, but one man, with binoculars to his eyes, said, "No, it just tipped, but he's out of the boat. I think he tried to cut too close to the island and got hung up on the bottom."

At the window now, Kimberly stared at the distant cluster of sails. One close to the island that marked the turning point in the race was sharply tilted, almost far enough to cause the boat to ship water. But the distance was too great, and she could see little detail.

"Is he overboard?" she asked anxiously of the man with the binoculars.

"No, he's standing in shallow water trying to push the boat back away from the island, but the wind is in the sail. Ah, now his partner is taking in the sail. They'll be all right. But they're not going to win the race. That's a shame too; there was only one boat ahead of them before they got hung up."

Kimberly breathed a sigh of relief and moved away from the window, but she had no desire to rejoin Hawke and the two women at the table. She was, in fact, relieved that she had had an excuse to leave them, for Hawke's mood was unfathomable, his strange coolness not only perplexing but adding to her own despondency. Moving toward the bar, she stopped to talk with several people and then wandered into the salon where she stayed, visiting at the various tables until the cheering from the bar informed her that the winner of the race had arrived back at the finish line.

Kimberly was not surprised that the winner was Bailey with the very efficient girl he had chosen to be his crew. She went out to congratulate him and then waited until the others had returned before gratefully saying good-bye to the boaters and going home, to rest and later to dress for the evening's dinner dance at which the trophy would be presented.

CHAPTER 13

Kimberly lingered on the porch when she reached her house. A quiet peace hung over the old town, except for the voice of the mockingbird who sat on a roof across the street, leaping madly in the air as he went through his repertoire. The streets were shielded from the breeze by the high bluff on the western side of town. The trees shading the streets were motionless in the soft air that was warmed and drenched with sunshine and exuded an intoxicating aroma that meant spring was in full flower. The streets were deserted except for an artist who sat before his easel painting one of the old buildings. To Kimberly there was something bittersweet about the loveliness of the perfect day, in vivid contrast to the emotions within her. During the long week that Hawke had avoided her, Kimberly had still hoped that no decision had been made; she had waited with thin patience to learn what he would finally decide to do. Now his cool silence of the morning had convinced her that her hopes were groundless; he would take the marina, and when his business here was finished, he would leave. Anger and heartbreak clamored within her at the knowledge; her way of life would be cut out from under her, and she wondered if she would ever be heart-whole again. When Hawke left, a part of her would go with him.

She was a fool, she told herself wearily, as she turned to go into the house; a fool and an idiot, and she wondered how all this had happened to her.

Although sleep would be impossible, Kimberly decided to rest, for the evening would be long. As she lay across her bed listening to the tireless arias of the mocker who continued his hopeful singing, she pictured his hopping flight, up and down, up and down, knowing he could go on like that far into the night, seemingly without ever needing rest.

It was late afternoon when Kimberly slowly awoke, her mind blank as she drifted up from layers of sleep. When she finally opened her eyes, her thoughts were slow to organize themselves, her memory dull, groping, and disconnected. When awareness flooded back, she sat up swiftly, instinctively aware that she had been asleep for long hours. Her eyes flew to the clock on the bedside table. It was five thirty! How could she have possibly slept so long? She had to be back on the Side Wheel before eight.

As she hurried downstairs to see if Richard had come home, Kimberly realized that she felt better than she had for more than a week. Nothing had changed, but the dismal unhappiness she had taken to bed with her had somewhat abated. With her physical well-being restored, her mental attitude had also improved. Even the fact that Richard was not in the house neither surprised nor overly upset her. She decided she would bathe and dress leisurely and be at her radiant best for the evening.

By seven thirty Kimberly was admiring herself before the full-length mirror on her door. Her dress was a burnt apricot, her favorite color, of softly clinging material with a gathered skirt that reduced her waist to nothingness. Although it was sleeveless, the dress had a tiny jacket. Mascara and eye shadow gave her eyes a wide, fawnlike softness, and a touch of rouge brightened

181

her cheeks. Her mood had changed since the morning, and when the doorbell rang, announcing Barry's arrival, she felt ready to face Hawke's cool disinterest and Laurie's jealous spite. Any dregs of gloom that still lurked in her mind were pushed back and overlaid with a buoyant assurance that all was not lost yet.

The boys had constructed a walkway of floats across the harbor from the land to the Side Wheel so that the guests would not have to walk the long way around to the boat. It was guarded on both sides by handrails and, as Kimberly and Barry reached the top of the steps near the marine store, she was gratified to see the number of people already there. The extra people from other marinas, who paid to attend, would defray the cost of what would otherwise have been a very expensive dinner.

The heat of the day had dissipated with the setting sun, but there was still a mellow warmth in the air where the watery smell of the river mingled with the perfume of the women. A full moon rose in the eastern sky, reflecting a silvery path along the river, and from the windows of the boat a glow of warm light spilled onto the harbor and dock. Later some people would dance on the outside deck,

Kimberly knew. Slipping through the side doors, they would dance in the moonlight to the muted strains of the music that drifted from the salon. Soft murmurs of endearment would be exchanged by those in love, and also by those who were merely in love with love and enchanted by the magic of the moonlight on the river and the distant music drifting on the mellow air.

Such thoughts made Kimberly's high spirits waver, but she quickly brushed them aside. It was a night to enjoy, and the confidence engendered by her long, restful sleep must not be endangered by fruitless daydreams.

A ripple of conversation reached her before she even stepped into the salon, a happy sound of people bent on enjoying themselves. She was entranced when she saw the old salon flooded with light from glowing chandeliers and alive with people. The women's gowns and the men's dark suits seemed to recreate the past and bring to life the bygone era when this room had been in its glory. The colors of the women's gowns – rose, butter-yellow, green, and soft blue – were like a bright mosaic reflected in the pier-glass mirrors. The flash and sparkle of gold from the women's jewelry and the heavy frames seemed to scintillate in the lights, and there was busy movement as people gathered in

183

groups, then drifted to other groups, or broke away to greet new arrivals. At the far end of the room the orchestra emitted disembodied sounds that indicated it was tuning up.

Even as Kimberly stood quietly appreciating the scene before her, she was alert for the sight of Hawke or Laurie and after several moments she was certain that they had not yet arrived. Then one of the Coreys called to her, and she was drawn into the crowd.

The orchestra finished their rasping, tuneless noises and soft dinner music drifted through the room just as a waiter announced that dinner would be served in ten minutes. Kimberly and Barry had just sat down at a table with Julie and Craig Dutton and their friends the Caswells, when Kimberly saw Hawke and Laurie. They were already joining the Coreys and Martha Lansing several tables away. Kimberly was so vividly aware of Hawke that she missed a question Craig asked.

"I asked if Phil won the race last year," he repeated.

"Yes, and the year before too. If he goes on like this, he's either going to be a terrific challenge to the others, or they'll all feel beaten before they start."

Barry had been watching her as she stared

at Hawke, and to avoid looking at him, she let her eyes drift past Craig's shoulder only to encounter the brilliant, knowing gaze of Luke Steed, who sat at the next table. Anger and annoyance rose in her, not so much at Steed and Barry as at herself for being so transparent. Well, she decided, she would make a point of ignoring Hawke. And why should she do otherwise, she thought. He had made no attempt even to smile at her. She turned, eager to join the conversation at her own table.

The meal was served by waiters in stiff white coats and black trousers. There was rib roast, fluffy whipped potatoes, delicate green asparagus tips, and a salad. A red wine accompanied the meal, the choice of which Kimberly had left to Barry. The food from his restaurant was always good, but he had surpassed himself with this meal, and Kimberly appreciated it, smiling fondly as she thanked him.

At the end of the meal Kimberly presented the trophy to Phil Bailey amid congratulations and laughing complaints about not giving anyone else a chance, and promises that next year would be different. As the waiters cleared the tables the orchestra struck up dance music, the bar was opened for those who preferred drinking to dancing, and the

185

groups who had each been sequestered at their own tables during the meal began to break up as couples moved to the dance floor or toward the bar.

The music was a combination of old and new, and Kimberly found herself dancing continuously as one partner after another claimed her. She was enjoying herself, realizing how long it had been since she had danced or gone to a party. Although she was purposely making no attempt to notice Hawke – neither where he was nor what he was doing – her glance was caught and held as Laurie drifted by in his arms, her delicate blond beauty enhanced by a soft blue gown, her perfect features emphasized by the fall of her pale hair in waves and curls from high at the back of her head. Her face was tilted up, her eyes on Hawke's face, and her lips smiling. But as Kimberly's glance moved to Hawke her eyes met his dark ones, and something electric seemed to flash between them. She almost lost the beat of the music as her breath caught somewhere deep inside her. She dragged her eyes away from his magnetic gaze, turning quickly to speak to Craig, not really aware of what she said but needing the diversion of his conversation.

Craig was leading her from the dance floor when Hawke's hand touched her arm. "This is our dance," he said, smiling down at her.

Kimberly returned his smile casually. As his arm went around her she noticed how tanned his smooth face looked against the white of his shirt. As he drew her close his eyes seemed to look deep into hers with a probing, assessing look, but she maintained an impersonal smile and stared back calmly at him, determined not to let him disconcert her with his sudden interest.

"At times like this I feel bad all over again about not owning the Side Wheel," she told him. "Can't you just feel the atmosphere?"

He nodded. "And I like the music. You're wise not to have one of those loud, guitar-strumming bands in a place like this."

"I thought so too. It just wouldn't fit. But some of the kids think this music is too old-fashioned."

"They might understand if they knew how old-fashioned you are."

"I'm not," she said indignantly, uncertain if his remark was meant as a compliment but feeling it was not.

"Smooth your feathers. What's wrong with being old-fashioned? Old-fashioned girls are a dying breed. I think the government should do something about it. After all, they shed tears about the lost passenger pigeons and the fate of the buffalo and the wolf. Why not give a little of that concern to girls? The old-fashioned girl is becoming almost as extinct."

"Well, I don't think I qualify for that category."

"Oh, but you do. You have all the old-fashioned virtues."

"Oh, you resent virtues," she accused with a flash of asperity.

"Not resent, really. I just find them piquant."

She suspected he was teasing, but his choice of subject was unwelcome in view of some of her past experiences with him, and she looked back stormily into his laughing eyes.

"And sometimes I not only find it piquant but quite attractive," he said softly as he drew her yet closer. She felt his chin against her temple as they danced, his breath gently stirring her hair.

What is he doing? she asked herself. *Why, after ignoring me for so long, is he talking like this?* Bugles of warning sounded in her mind. She could not permit him to break through her defenses. Never again could she allow him to know how much he meant to her, nor let him suspect that his very nearness set her nerves quivering and her heart pounding. She tried to relax, to forget his baiting and the look he had given her when he first took her in his arms. She concentrated on the soft strains of the old song they were playing. It was a haunting melody, romantic and sad, and she could not immediately identify it. Then some of the words came back to her: "I love you. I love you. That's all that I can say." Oh, what were the other lines? The melody was so haunting and the words seemed meant for her. It was truly all she could say. No matter how foolish she was, in view of her anger and occasional dislike of Hawke, it always came back to the same thing: She loved him.

The sad strains of the song ended, and Hawke stepped back to look down at her, his arms still around her. There was a slight smile on his lips that slowly died as he looked into her face, and Kimberly, lost to the bustle of couples leaving the dance floor as the musicians deserted their instruments for a short break, stared back solemnly at him.

The annoyance in Laurie's voice cut through the magical moment. "Let's go into the bar for a drink," she said, her venomous glance lighting momentarily on Kimberly. "All this dancing makes me thirsty."

As Kimberly turned, Hawke's hands fell away from her. "Right," he said to Laurie. To Kimberly he said, "Old-fashioned girls are often romantics too." And tucking Laurie's hand into the crook of his elbow, he moved toward the bar.

Kimberly followed his retreating back with wide, questioning eyes. Somehow she had given herself away. But how? She had no idea, but Hawke was aware of the emotions aroused in her by the strains of the sad music. Oh, damn the man! It was almost as if he could read her mind. Nothing she thought was safe from him.

The guests lingered long, obviously enjoying themselves, but Hawke did not again ask Kimberly for a dance, nor did he come near her. Laurie was by his side constantly. The rest of the evening dragged for Kimberly – the evening that had begun with so much pleasure but had been ruined, or at least dampened, by the short time she had spent in Hawke's arms.

By the time the last guests said good-bye, it was the small hours of the morning, and Kimberly was again weary, not merely from the late hours but from the effort she had had to make to sustain an appearance of gaiety. She was grateful that the dinner dance had been a rousing success. If she managed to retain control of the marina, it could only be an asset to future business.

CHAPTER 14

During the following week Hawke was as elusive as he had been the week before, and Kimberly remained uninformed about his plans for the marina. The waiting and uncertainty were becoming more and more unbearable, and by Saturday she wished she had broached the subject the night of the dinner dance when she had an opportunity to talk with him. But she had mooned away that opportunity, listening to the music and talking trivialities. Hawke and Laurie were gone again today, but she decided to seek him out when she returned and ask pointed questions. Waiting was no longer tolerable, even though Barry had assured her that he had seen nothing in any of the legal papers about a foreclosure on the marina.

It had been a busy day, with crowds of people gathering at the marina and the Side Wheel serving food at all hours for the hungry boaters. Kimberly was thankful for the constant distractions. Phil Bailey arrived with several friends and, when they returned after a long day on the river, he insisted that Kimberly join them for dinner on the Side Wheel. Reluctant to leave the marine store at first, Kimberly finally decided that she needed the rest. The other two men were attractive, and Phil quickly gathered two other girls for their party, but Kimberly found herself unable to take part in the gaiety and was finally sorry she had joined them.

Eventually the guests drifted away, and at ten o'clock closing time she thankfully said good-bye to Phil and his friends.

Mr. Glass had arrived long before; the boys had finished their work and gone home; and still Kimberly lingered, finding small tasks with which to occupy herself until she was so weary, she decided to return to the Side Wheel for a cup of coffee while she kept vigil.

Moonlight streamed through the wide windows where Kimberly sat with an unwanted cup of coffee on the table before her. With the white moon bright on the water and the islands mysteriously black it was a night for romance. Hawke and Laurie could have lingered at any port along the way, perhaps even planned to stay the night wherever they were. The thought made Kimberly hate Laurie and hate Hawke even more. She kept telling herself that she was a fool, but still she was unable to force herself to go home to what she knew would be a sleepless bed.

Somewhere in the air was the fragrance of wood smoke, and Kimberly realized she had been smelling it for some time. She sniffed appreciatively, for there was often that sweet, heady odor drifting through the streets of Elsah. Suddenly she stiffened, turning swiftly to look into the darkened room where pale, swirling smoke, reflecting the moonlight, billowed toward her from the far end of the kitchen. Without wasting a thought on the exit so close beside her, Kimberly rushed across the room toward the door to the interior, her only thought being to find the fire and extinguish it before it was out of control. But as she swung open the door to the salon a thick pall of smoke engulfed her. She reeled back, coughing and choking. Through streaming eyes she tried to find the source of the fire but there was only the opaque, enveloping smoke, forcing her back the way she had come until she had to flee across the kitchen to the landward exit.

As she dashed around the open side deck she could hear Mr. Glass calling to her, his voice raised in desperation.

"I'm here," she answered when she reached the back deck. "Where's the fire?"

He had boarded the boat and was on the starboard deck, opposite to where she had come out of the kitchen. At the sound of her voice he turned and hurried along the side of the boat toward her. "Let's get out of here before this burns to the waterline," he called, waving her toward her outboard, which he had evidently used to reach the Side Wheel and was now tied alongside.

"We have to try to put out the fire," she told him.

"It's all through the bar already and moving into the salon. There's nothing we can do."

Looking forward, Kimberly could see the red glare of the windows, which were already popping and shattering with the heat. It was an old boat, mostly wood, and would burn fast, but surely they could not stand idly by and watch it being destroyed!

Then there were voices calling across the water, and several boats approached from the river, nosing into the narrow channel that led to the harbor. Kimberly decided they must have seen the fire from across the river, where there were several large marinas, and come to help. They boarded swiftly, their buckets on long ropes that they dropped into the water and dragged back, full and dripping.

"Get some buckets and help," one of them shouted. "The fireboat is coming any minute."

Mr. Glass was slow, but Kimberly ran to the back deck, returning in minutes with a bucket for each of them. As she dropped her bucket into the water she glanced with frantic eyes toward the salon, where flames were licking out of the windows and reaching up the outer side of the boat. Smoke rolled out with the flames. The fire's roar drowned the calls of the men, and somewhere a siren sounded, growing louder. The whole scene was lighted by a red glare that made the men's frantic efforts look like an eerie dance. Kimberly dashed the water from her bucket through one of the open windows, heard a quickly submerged hiss, and knew that their puny efforts were hopeless.

Then the men were shouting at her and waving her back, scrambling down into their small boats that bobbed along the side of the Side Wheel. She turned to see the fireboat, its siren wailing to silence. Almost immediately its hose shot a strong stream of water toward the flaming windows as the man at the helm tacked it closer to the Side Wheel.

Kimberly and Mr. Glass hurried into her outboard, pushed away from the Side Wheel and, using an oar, moved farther out into the harbor, where they sat watching the efforts of the fireboat crew.

It was hopeless. As quickly as they had come, it had not been soon enough, for fire raged through most of the lower deck now. Only the kitchen appeared untouched.

The men who first arrived were also watching from their boats, one very close to Kimberly's. "We saw the fire from across the river," one of the men said, raising his voice to be heard above the sounds of the fire and the roaring hose. "They might still be able to save it. You know, this is the first time we've ever used the fireboat."

Kimberly recalled having heard that one of the large marinas slightly upriver had bought a fireboat the year before. Watching it now, she could see that it pumped a huge volume of water, and a faint hope glimmered in her that Barry would be able to salvage something from this disaster.

Two hours later they all stood on the docks looking off across the harbor to where the crew of the fireboat were still pouring water into the Side Wheel. The flames were gone now and only the long, scorched marks extending above each blackened window testified to the holocaust that had raged within. Two men, dragging the extendable fire hose, had boarded the boat and were moving from window to window, drenching the interior so that no vagrant smoldering coal could start the blaze again.

The rolling smoke, rising like a beacon into the clear sky, had attracted others, and a small crowd had gathered along the docks, watching the men aboard the Side Wheel. All the marina lights had been turned on now. In their bright glare Kimberly recognized some people from other marinas, but there were strangers too, passersby on the River Road, and those from downriver whose homes were perched high on the bluffs with long, broad views of the river. They talked together in quiet voices but with the subdued excitement that always accompanies a catastrophe.

Kimberly stood among them, aware of the surge of their voices but intent on the boat across the water, thinking what a loss this would be for Barry and wondering how well he was insured. She thought sadly, too, of the beautiful salon that was no more.

"Are you all right?"

She started slightly at the touch on her arm and the voice close to her ear, and looking up, saw Hawke peering down into her face, his brows drawn together in a frown, his eyes examining her intently.

"Were you aboard when the fire started?"

Kimberly stared at him in surprise,

197

wondering how he came to be here, for there was no possible way he could have passed in his cruiser without being seen.

"Yes, but I'm all right," she told him. "How did you get here?"

"I tied up over there." He motioned toward the small cove at their left just within the entrance to the harbor. There was a tiny pier where boaters often tied up to picnic on the grassy verge beyond.

"You're sure you're all right?" Hawke persisted.

"Yes." Her eyes were back on the men on the Side Wheel and she realized that they would be finished soon. After working long hours, they would appreciate coffee and perhaps a drink, but she had nothing to offer them.

"I have to go home and make some coffee," she said. "I should have something for those men when they finish." She turned away from Hawke.

"They can come aboard the *Pandora*," Hawke told her. "We'll make some coffee there."

"Mr. Glass?" Kimberly turned to the old man who was standing beside her.

"I'll tell them," he assured her. "You go now."

198

Hawke's hand was on Kimberly's elbow as she allowed herself to be led beyond the marine store and around the near end of the harbor to the cruiser that was moored at the inadequate dock there.

There were hurrying footsteps behind them, and Laurie called petulantly, "You could have told me you were going back to the *Pandora*."

There was no welcome in Hawke's voice as he said, "We are going to make some coffee for those men. We will not need your help, Laurie."

Kimberly was hardly aware of the resentment on the girl's face, for after hours of tension she felt herself trembling slightly as weakness enveloped her.

Aboard the *Pandora*, Hawke led her to a chair, then turned to the liquor cabinet, and quickly poured a glass half full.

"Drink that," he said, handing it to Kimberly. "It's brandy."

Obediently she took a quick gulp and immediately choked.

"Drink more," he said as she tried to hand the glass back to him. "You look like you need it. I'll put on some water; they'll have to be happy with instant coffee, if that's what they want, but I imagine most of them will opt for a drink."

He was right, for when Mr. Glass brought the men aboard, several took beers and the others straight whiskey. There were seven of them besides Mr. Glass, and they crowded the cabin, not taking seats because they were all grimed with smoke and soot. They were exhilarated by the evening's excitement and pleased with themselves for having saved the Side Wheel.

"It looks pretty bad inside," one of them remarked. "I hope that guy Mead has fire insurance."

"Yeah," another agreed. "Almost the whole lower deck is gutted, and there might be damage to the upper deck too. Even if the fire didn't get through the ceiling, it was on fire."

They accepted another drink and then left, Mr. Glass going with them, assuring Kimberly as he left that he would turn out the lights and keep an eye on the Side Wheel during the night. "Just in case," he said.

It seemed very quiet when they had gone and Kimberly, still sipping the brandy, felt a rush of exhaustion after the release of the tension she had been under. The little work she had actually done could hardly cause such lassitude.

Thinking of the grimy appearance of the men, she had looked for the first time at her own clothes and discovered that her white slacks were dark with a silting of soot, her blouse smoke-stained and her hands black. Now she cautiously started to rise, taking care not to touch the fabric of the armchair in which she sat, but Hawke pushed her back gently with a hand on her shoulder.

"Just rest a little longer. You look like you did all the work yourself."

"But I hardly did anything," she protested. "After the fireboat came, I just sat in my outboard and then stood on the dock. I don't know why I'm so weak."

"It's a reaction to all that adrenaline shooting through your system. Were you aboard when the fire started?"

"I was in the kitchen, and I didn't even know the boat was on fire until I smelled the smoke. By that time the whole bar was burning."

While Kimberly told him what had happened, he soaked a bar towel with water from the carafe and leaned above her, holding her head with one hand while he wiped the grime from her face.

"You're as pale as I thought you were," he said, examining her critically as he ministered to her as to a child.

Until this moment, too lost to be fully aware, Kimberly suddenly recalled their parting that morning almost two weeks ago, his taunts and her own anger and bitterness. It hardly seemed possible that he was the same man who had leered down at her from the rail of his boat while Laurie disappeared into the cabin behind him.

"I can do it," she said, reaching for the towel, feeling suddenly foolish and very aware of his nearness.

Releasing the towel, he sank into a nearby chair and, as Kimberly finished wiping her face and scrubbing her grimy hands, she felt his dark eyes watching her. She became acutely aware of how alone they were in the cabin of his boat.

"I'll have to go," she finally said into the long silence, her voice sounding breathless to her own ears.

He was on his feet immediately. "I'll take you home."

"I have to have my car so I can drive back in the morning."

They were standing facing each other and suddenly his hand came up and stroked the side of her face, his eyes somber as they gazed into hers. "I'm glad nothing happened to you," he said.

A clamoring fear rose in Kimberly, warning her to hurry away. If he took her in his arms, she would be lost. She was too tired to fight him, her mind too dulled with strain to resist the wild, surging thrill of his nearness. But his hand was on her elbow, turning her to the door so suddenly that she was on the deck before she even realized that her rising panic was pointless.

"I'll drive behind you to be sure you get home safely," he told her when they reached the parking lot.

Although she insisted it was not necessary, he was behind her all the way to the driveway. Her mind hammered with indecision: Should she ask him in? and if she did, what if Richard was gone again? Yet how could she just say good-bye and leave him when he had been so kind?

All her worries proved useless when she pulled into the driveway beside her house, and Hawke, without even turning off the engine of his car, merely slowed and waved to her before driving around the next corner. Kimberly felt deserted.

CHAPTER 15

It was late when Kimberly drove to the marina the next morning, for she had slept the sleep of utter exhaustion, not waking until long after her usual time. During a quick breakfast of coffee and toast her mind had been on practical matters. She would have to install a refrigerator in the marine shack, she had decided, for though the kitchen on the Side Wheel had been spared, the fire might have been started by faulty wiring, so it would be impossible to use the electrical appliances there. For today she would take a sandwich along for lunch, and needing extra time to make it, she hurried even more, gulping the last of the coffee and almost choking on the toast.

She was on the River Road, the bluffs towering on her left and a silken blue sky sparkling above, reflected in a darker blue on the water, before the need to hurry left her. With time to relax, the memory of the night before came back and with it the ever-present thought of Hawke. He was as changeable as a chameleon and his inconsistency kept her forever off balance. He was not at all the kind of man she wanted to love. After ignoring her for practically two weeks, he had suddenly shown warm concern for her. Still, she knew he would not hesitate if he decided to take the marina away from them. But new hope rose in her as she recalled that he wanted the Side Wheel too. With the Side Wheel burned, he might change his mind about wanting the marina, for there could be no clubhouse for his customers, and he had been quite emphatic about wanting that.

As soon as she stopped in the parking lot she saw the curiosity-seekers lined along the deck of the Side Wheel, staring through the broken windows at the inside of the boat. Well, she could hardly blame them. She was anxious herself to see what damage had been done.

Minutes later she was looking through the broken windows with appalled wonder at the blackened cavelike interior and wondering how the men, with only one hose, had ever managed to put out the fire. The tables and chairs in the salon were gone, crumbled into charred ruins. Only the marble tops, although smoke-blackened, were still recognizable. Glancing at the ceiling, she saw that all the lovely carved beams were either gone or burned beyond recognition. A feeling of loss swept over Kimberly as she looked at the pitiful remains of the once elegant salon. It could not be replaced.

Moving along the side deck, she saw that only fragments of the partition between the salon and the bar remained. Through the gaping wall she could see that the bar was even more damaged, if possible, than the salon. When she reached the foredeck where she could look directly into the bar, Kimberly gasped in surprise, for the floor was burned through, a large gaping hole showing the interior of the hull, black and cracking. Over everything there was still the damp gleam of water and the strong smell of wet, burned wood. If she had held any hope that Barry would be able to salvage the boat, it faded at the sight of this total destruction. True, the outer walls were intact; but the interior was gutted and the cost of repairing it would be prohibitive, especially considering that the restaurant had made little money over the costs of operating it. The men from the fireboat had said the kitchen was not burned, and now Kimberly moved around the outer deck, wondering if this could possibly be true.

Barry saw her through the window at the same time that she saw him, and she moved to the door. As she entered Kimberly's eyes went from his troubled face to the kitchen and saw at once that though there had been no fire here, everything in the kitchen was smoke-stained, the area around the door to the salon black.

"It looks like this is the only part of this deck that's left," Barry said.

"I'm so sorry, Barry. Did you have fire insurance?"

"Yes. They want to find out how it started, but I'm not worried about that."

Kimberly looked at him questioningly, for it was obvious that something was worrying him. Instead of explaining, he said, "Let's go to the marine store; it's too dirty in here to sit down."

They sat at the small desk in the corner of the marine store, and Kimberly studied Barry's troubled face as she waited for him to speak. There was something more than the burning of the boat on his mind.

"What is it, Barry?" she finally asked with a tinge of impatience. His reluctance to speak had sparked a formless dread in her, making her certain that she was in some way involved in his problem.

"Kimberly, I hate to say it. I feel like a heel. It's just that I think you should know now. Well, I mean I don't like to do anything without letting you know first."

"Know what?"

He was fingering a stapler that he had picked up from the desk, opening the top arm and clicking it back in place repeatedly. In the silence the clicking was loud and nerve-racking to Kimberly.

"You know the Side Wheel wasn't making money?" he asked.

"Yes. Yes, you told me that."

207

"Now. . . . You know I wanted to wait until Hawke was gone. . . ." He hesitated, looking at her as if asking if Hawke would ever be gone, but Kimberly merely waited, her impatience held in check.

"Kimberly, if he still wants to buy, I'll almost have to sell. There isn't any point in my trying to rebuild it and now I won't be able to find many people who will want to buy it."

"You're trying to tell me that if Hawke still wants to buy the Side Wheel, you would like to sell it to him."

"Yes." His blue eyes were almost tragic as they looked into hers, and besides the apology there, she read a hope of forgiveness.

"But, Barry, I told you before, I wanted you to sell if you could. You were the one who insisted on waiting. If Hawke still wants the boat, of course you'll have to sell it to him."

Even as she said it Kimberly felt a sinking feeling, for Barry's refusal to sell the old steamer had been like a short reprieve. Once Hawke had the boat, there would be no reason for him to wait any longer before acquiring the marina.

The ringing of the telephone forestalled anything more that might have been said, and Kimberly picked it up automatically, saying, "Cartwright's Landing."

208

"Oh, Kimberly, I'm so glad you're there." The voice was so excited, so drawn with stress that at first Kimberly failed to recognize it as Mrs. Kramer's. "It's Richard. I called an ambulance, but they haven't come yet." She hurried on, almost tripping over her words. "I have to go back to him. I think it's a stroke. I can't move him."

"I'll be right there." She slammed down the receiver without waiting for an answer and, snatching her purse from the desk, dashed from the store. "It's Dad," she called over her shoulder to Barry.

As she swung out of the parking lot she saw Barry hurrying to his own car and, through the haze of worry that enveloped her, she was thankful that he would be there to help her. Mrs. Kramer had sounded distraught to the point of hysteria.

As Kimberly brought her car to a screeching halt before the house, she could see Richard stretched out on the porch, appearing limp and lifeless. Mrs. Kramer, who had been hovering over him, hurried across the sidewalk, talking as she came. "He hasn't moved since he fell there, but I can feel his heart beating, so he isn't dead."

Kimberly rushed past the woman and knelt on the porch beside her father, hardly aware of the rough cement that grated her knees even through her slacks. There was a sagging limpness about Richard's pale face that frightened her.

"What makes you think it's a stroke?" she asked, wondering if it could have been a heart attack.

"His face. When I saw him fall, I thought it was a heart attack, but his face is so dragged down on that one side. I was in my front garden when he came out of the house. First he staggered and fell against that post, and then he just slipped down."

Barry, who had been right behind Kimberly all the way to the house, asked, "Do you want me to take him into the house, Kimberly?"

"No, I don't think so. It might be better not to try to move him." Then, glancing at his legs, she added, "But his leg is bent under him. Do you think it might be broken?"

"He slid down that post so easy, I don't see how he could have broke it," Mrs. Kramer told them. "It might be best to straighten it, though."

"I don't know," Kimberly said, uncertain. "What do you do for a stroke?"

Neither of them knew.

It seemed an eternity before they heard the distant wail of the ambulance.

Kimberly rode in the ambulance, watching

as the attendant put an oxygen mask over Richard's face, took his blood pressure and pulse, and then merely watched and waited as they sped toward the hospital in Alton, the siren screaming. Kimberly watched Richard's face, noting his strangely distorted mouth, and wondering if he had had a stroke. Behind them, through the rear window, she noticed that Barry followed close in the wake of the ambulance. His presence made her feel less alone with the terrible dread that Richard might not recover.

Barry stayed with her in the waiting room at the hospital during the whole of the afternoon, for which Kimberly was grateful, knowing that the endless waiting would be unendurable if she had to keep the vigil alone. Shortly after their arrival, a doctor had stopped to tell her that it was a stroke, but they were as yet unable to assess the damage.

"Was it a bad one?" Kimberly asked with frightened eyes.

"I'm afraid it was. You can see him now if you care to, but he's still unconscious."

He hardly seemed like Richard, lying there so quietly, the sheet smoothed to his chin, the white pillow unwrinkled as if he had not moved since being placed there. Kimberly lingered only a short time, returning to pace the waiting room floor after only five minutes.

211

Once Barry suggested that she go home and return in the evening, but Kimberly refused, determined to be there when Richard regained consciousness. During the long afternoon she divided her time between visits to his silent room, where Richard always looked exactly the same, and pacing the corridors and waiting room with Barry always at her side.

During the early evening Hawke arrived. By then her tension was so great that she welcomed his appearance as a much needed diversion. It seemed that she had spent an eternity in the sterile atmosphere of the hospital, a place unpleasant to her at any time but becoming more and more distasteful as the hours dragged past.

She had not forgotten her distrust of Hawke, but preferred, at this moment, to recall only his gentle consideration of the night before. And although she refused to let the thought surface in her mind, she needed him, needed him in a way she would never need Barry. His very presence seemed to bolster her sagging hopes. She greeted him with a far warmer welcome than she realized.

"How is he?" His voice was solemn, with none of the mockery he so often indulged in.

"We don't know, Hawke. We just keep waiting. It was a stroke, and he's still unconscious. We've been waiting all day."

Barry had said nothing, but Kimberly was unaware of this, for they had been silent for long hours before Hawke's arrival. Everything they had to say had been said in the first hours. Now she told Hawke about Mrs. Kramer's call and the trip to the hospital.

"I'm sorry I wasn't here." It was not an apology, merely a statement. Looking at him, Kimberly noticed for the first time that the white slacks and blue-and-white shirt were similar to what he usually wore aboard the cruiser. She wondered suddenly if he had only just returned and come directly to the hospital without even taking time to shower and change. Then, noticing the dark shadow of a beard on his face, she was certain of this, and a weak happiness engulfed her, the first carefree thought she had had since Mrs. Kramer's call.

It was past nine when Richard finally regained consciousness. He had been drugged heavily, and Kimberly watched in horror when he tried to speak, and the right side of his face refused to obey his wishes, remaining still and downdrawn so that his words were garbled. She refused to leave until he drifted into a natural sleep, and then was unable to find the doctor to question him. Another doctor, one she had not seen before, told her it would take time to discover how much permanent damage there would be. Even after he was well enough to leave the hospital, there could be some improvement, so nothing could be definitely known. They would just have to wait and see.

The long wait was over. Feeling more weary than she believed possible, Kimberly walked between the two men, out the doors, and down the steps of the hospital. Nothing had been said by any of them as they traversed the halls, but now at the foot of the steps Hawke's hand was on Kimberly's as he said, "I might as well take Kimberly home. There's no need for you to drive all the way out there."

Kimberly came out of her lethargy long enough to notice the slight awkwardness as Barry stood undecided, obviously preferring to take her home himself. But Hawke was already turning her toward his car and raising a hand in a good-bye motion to Barry. His tone of voice had been decisive with a note of dismissal for Barry, making it impossible for him to do other than acquiesce.

"Good-bye, Barry, and thank you so much," Kimberly told him, turning from Hawke and taking his hand. "I don't know what I would have done without you." She could feel sorry for Barry, knowing the

214

helplessness he must be feeling at Hawke's casual arrogance.

Kimberly and Hawke were silent as they drove through the twilight, Kimberly idly scanning the river ahead as the road wound along its edge, her eyes not really seeing it, her thoughts unfocused and wandering. The release from tension after the day-long wait had resulted in a deep apathy, and she sat torpid and listless as the miles passed, neither speaking nor aware of Hawke's own silence.

CHAPTER 16

Hawke did not leave her at her door, nor did he wait for an invitation to come in. Taking her key, he ushered her into the house.

"Have you eaten?" he asked after closing the door behind them.

"Uh, I had a sandwich sometime today," Kimberly told him, trying to recall exactly when that was.

"But no dinner." It was not a question, and taking her arm, he led her to the kitchen. "Sit down there," he ordered, moving one of the Windsor chairs back from the table.

"I can fix something," Kimberly told him, but he forced her gently into the chair.

"Just sit there and rest."

From behind the partition she heard water running into a coffeepot, the soft hiss of the refrigerator door being opened, followed by the rattle and bang of drawers and cabinets being opened and closed. Within a remarkably short time he was back with a sandwich on a plate. As he placed it before her Kimberly stared at it, first in amazement and then in doubt, for it was so immense, she wondered if she could possibly open her mouth wide enough to accommodate it. He had apparently used everything in the refrigerator. For the first time that day Kimberly laughed.

"If I'm going to even try to eat it, I'm going to have to cut it into smaller pieces," she told him. Looking up she saw that Hawke, too, was smiling.

"It seems that even the sight of food makes you feel better," he said. "I'll get the coffee."

She was ravenously hungry, she discovered, and even before she had finished the sandwich, the apathy that held her was disappearing. Even her utter exhaustion was washed away by cup after cup of strong coffee.

As Kimberly came back to herself, her awareness of Hawke increased, and with it came a confusing uncertainty. To her the

216

kindness and consideration he was displaying were foreign to his arrogant nature, yet both last night and today he had been considerate of her. Tonight her normally ambivalent feelings towards him were almost forgotten, soothed away in the comfort she took in his presence.

"You're tired," he said, interrupting her thoughts. "I'll leave and let you go to bed."

"I'm not tired. I mean, I know I can't sleep. I'm just weary. Waiting is more exhausting than a hard day's work. But I'm too worried to sleep." She was eager to keep him with her, reluctant to be left alone with the darting fear that Richard might never recover, and the dismal prospect of the future if he did not.

Hawke was on his feet ready to leave, but he stood looking quietly down at her, his tanned face without expression, his black eyes a perfect mask for his thoughts. Kimberly gazed back at him, reluctant to ask him to stay and unaware that her own wide amber eyes, tragic and beseeching, told him more clearly than words that she wanted him here with her.

"Let's go into the other room," he said finally. "You can't relax on these straight chairs."

Hawke lit a small lamp in the corner of

217

the parlor as Kimberly sank wearily onto the couch.

"Lie down and try to rest," he suggested, taking an armchair at right angles to the couch.

Kimberly merely sat quietly, noting that the ashes were still in the hearth, left from the fire Hawke had kindled on that night that seemed so long ago. The sight of them brought back memories of the foolish hopes and plans she had made for that night. Looking back now, she knew that she had been naive to think that Hawke had only to know she loved him to make all her plans and dreams come true. Perhaps Laurie had told the truth, and he would marry her for her money, but Kimberly doubted it. She doubted that he would ever be willing to share himself and relinquish his freedom in something as binding as marriage. Exhausted and worried as she was, the thought that he would leave and she would never see him again brought a feeling of desolation. She was acutely aware of him in the chair beside her, but she kept her eyes downcast, fearful that if she looked at him, he would read in her face the despair and yearning she felt.

"You've had a bad couple of days, haven't you?" He was out of the chair, leaning toward her, his hand beneath her chin, lifting her face, forcing her to look at him. Their eyes met and held, and deep in his, Kimberly could see a flicker, a glow. As she stared back his hands were on her shoulders lifting her, drawing her close. A wild rush of excitement flooded her as he bent over her, his lips on hers in a long, ardent kiss. Though she leaned weakly into his arms, her lips soft beneath his, the memory of other kisses restrained her, and one tiny corner of her mind warned her to be cautious. Yet there was no way she could control the feeling of weak surrender that possessed her. Then Hawke was holding her in a close embrace, his cheek against hers, and she could hear his breathing close to her ear. If only she could stay here forever, forget all the things that plagued and worried her. And if only she were free to respond to his kisses as she longed to do, instead of being burdened by the fear that he would suddenly become different from what he seemed to be when he held her in his arms.

Then he was drawing away from her, his hands on her shoulders, smiling down into her face.

"You needed something to distract you," he told her, his eyes dancing with amusement.

Through her surprised disappointment Kimberly felt a rush of thankfulness that she had not allowed herself to be carried away.

"You mean the kiss was merely for therapeutic purposes?" she finally asked.

"More or less. Not that it wasn't enjoyable. But it served its purpose. You're looking more annoyed than worried, and you've stopped wringing your hands."

"It was very kind and thoughtful of you," she said primly with a touch of sarcasm, not returning his smile.

"Sit down. I want to tell you something." His hands on her shoulders forced her to sit down again on the couch. Seating himself beside her, her hands clasped in his, he continued, "I've seen other people with strokes. The crippling isn't necessarily permanent. There can be some rehabilitation. It takes time, and there might have to be therapy, but he won't stay the way he is now. And one thing you can be thankful for: His mind does not seem to have been affected."

He was being kind, Kimberly thought, and she should appreciate it, but she was still annoyed that the kiss had meant nothing to him.

"Do you understand?" he asked when she failed to answer him.

"I understand, but the doctors did say it was a bad stroke."

"But tearing yourself apart won't change a thing."

He was only half right, Kimberly thought, her eyes gazing sightlessly at the blue rug. It was as much her useless love for him that was tearing her apart as her desperate concern for Richard. Then his hand was on her cheek, gently brushing her hair back from her face, curving about the nape of her neck and drawing her toward him. Kimberly's hands went quickly to his chest, holding him away.

"I don't think I need any more therapy tonight," she said coolly, her amber eyes looking levelly into his dark ones.

His expression changed subtly, his hand on her neck tightening its hold, and for a moment Kimberly thought she could read in his expression a determination to take her in his arms whether she willed it or not. But his hands dropped away from her.

"You're right," he said, standing suddenly and looking down at her speculatively before he turned toward the door.

"You're leaving?" she asked quickly, hurrying after him.

"Yes. You said you've had enough therapy."

He was already opening the door and Kimberly found herself without words. She did not want him to go and leave her alone, but her pride held her silent as she murmured an awkward good night. As he crossed the sidewalk toward his car she called, "Thank you for bringing me home."

His only answer was a casual wave as he slid easily into the seat and started the motor. Kimberly watched the taillights until they disappeared around the corner.

CHAPTER 17

In the days that followed Kimberly divided her time between the marina and the hospital, often stopping in the morning, assigning work to the boys, spending some time doing the books, and then going to the hospital. Richard was showing improvement already, and now it was definite that his mind had not been affected by the stroke, although there was still paralysis on his right side. The doctor assured her that with therapy some of the crippling could be overcome but although he had hopes of some rehabilitation, he doubted complete recovery could be achieved. It was a stunning blow to know that he might never walk again, but after the fear that he might die or become a mere vegetable, it was almost welcome news.

There were many people, Kimberly assured herself, who lived full lives though confined to a wheelchair.

As she slowly accepted the fact that Richard would be crippled, and the worry about his immediate welfare lessened, Kimberly became more and more conscious of Hawke. He was often gone from the marina, the sight of the empty slip where his boat moored causing her an instant feeling of tension. Although she was usually certain Laurie was with him, she was constantly alert for a sign of the girl either on her own yacht or somewhere about the marina. Laurie had not confined herself to Hawke, for she had met other men, and when Hawke was away, either on his cruiser or in his rented car, she could be seen laughing and talking with them. Phil Bailey was obviously falling in love with her, but she was often the center of a group of men, laughing, flirting, and encouraging them all. Sometimes, watching her, Kimberly wondered how men could be so stupid. But perhaps they weren't stupid, only aware of her looks and unconcerned by the lack of character that lurked behind them. Phil certainly appeared to have good sense. He was the most active of her suitors, although he had trouble keeping her to himself. Kimberly could see the intent look in his eyes when

223

Hawke was near, for Hawke still had first claim on her attentions.

As for herself Kimberly knew she was jealous and often viewed Laurie sourly, wondering how any of them could find her attractive. To Kimberly she appeared shallow and spiteful, lacking even basic good manners and devoid of morals.

As for Hawke, she now viewed her past hopes of luring him into a proposal as the height of foolishness. He was a man who would never marry, never even let himself fall in love, not with her and not with Laurie. The wild yearning he had aroused in her was now a dull and constant ache. Although she longed to be with him, she wished, at the same time, that he would go away, out of her life, so that she would never have to see him again. With that thought came the renewed fear that he would take the marina from her, for now more than ever she needed the marina. With Richard at home and not well, there would be no way she could take a job in Alton or St. Louis and hope to support them. She had already spoken to Mrs. Kramer, asking if, when Richard came home, she could watch him during the day, make his meals, and see that he had whatever he needed. Ever ready to earn a little extra money, Mrs. Kramer had agreed with alacrity. The doctor had told her a

224

visiting nurse could come twice a week for his baths and anything else that had to be done, but the money the marina could earn, without the drain of Richard's gambling, was now a necessity. When Kimberly thought of this, the unwelcome feeling she had for Hawke turned to hatred, and these ambivalent feelings kept her in an emotional turmoil.

Hawke had neither sought her out again nor come to the hospital to visit Richard. At the marina he greeted her with a casual wave and usually had little to say to her. It was almost as if that evening in the parlor had been no more than a dream, and the kindness and consideration he had shown her, both that night and the night of the fire, only figments of her imagination.

Although Barry had no business to bring him to the marina since the Side Wheel was destroyed, he appeared the following Sunday. The crowds were increasing with the season, and Kimberly was busy, not only with the store and arrangements for the boys to do the extra work that many were requesting be done on their crafts, but with the social aspect of her position. Though Kimberly had· acted the role of hostess, the regular customers made many unnecessary demands on her time, seemingly unaware that she had other work to do. She had always encouraged this attitude graciously, feeling that it made the marina more personal than just a place to moor a boat. Her customers were greeted as welcome friends – and many of them were friends – their needs and problems being met with personal interest rather than businesslike expediency. But now with so much of her time spent at the hospital, Kimberly was finding herself rushed, assaulted on all sides with both socializing and the need to accomplish the necessary work.

"I've been so busy, Barry," she explained. "Can't we talk later?"

"It won't take long, but I have to talk to you now," he told her with a worried look.

With the Side Wheel uninhabitable there was nowhere to go but the marine store, and they could find no privacy there. Kimberly led him to the desk in the far corner, hoping that anyone who came in would see them in busy conversation and not interrupt.

Barry drew the extra chair close to the desk, his voice low as he said, "I sold the Side Wheel to Hawke. I couldn't pass up his offer, Kimberly. It might be the only one I'll ever get."

Kimberly nodded numbly. This meant that Hawke also intended to have the marina. All his kindness had meant nothing; he was still, as he had said, a businessman, and he took what he wanted without letting emotion sway him. But the disappointment, the anger, the dread feeling of desertion that came over her, made Kimberly realize how much she had actually believed that he would never do this to her. Her disappointment in him was almost as great as her fear of what the future would be without the marina.

"I'm sorry, Kimberly," Barry said, and she realized she had forgotten his presence.

"I don't blame you, Barry. I know you couldn't do anything else."

Slowly the heartbreak of knowing how little Hawke cared was replaced with simmering anger. He had used her ruthlessly, lulled her suspicions with kindness, and pretended concern while he went about destroying her life. Her rage was such that she yearned to hurt him even more. But he was impervious to injury, and she was helpless to do more than rant and rave, which would probably end by having to endure his arrogant laughter, and being reminded that he had warned her he took what he wanted.

Kimberly hardly knew how she parted from Barry. Somehow the late afternoon passed as she walked the gravel roads and the docks, trying to dissipate the tension that gripped her. People spoke to her and she answered,

227

a forced smile on her lips, but she made no attempt to do any work. Occasionally she returned to the marine store, only to discover that customers had helped themselves, leaving money and a note to tell her what they had bought.

It was dusk, and most of the boats had been moored, their owners having gone elsewhere – to a bar and restaurant several miles away – or taken themselves home earlier than usual. Kimberly saw Hawke's cruiser nosing into the harbor. She was on the gravel road near the foot of the steps to the parking lot when the craft passed, and she gazed back mutely as Laurie, on the foredeck, waved and smiled at her. She would have liked to go back to the marine store or even lock up and go home, but pride forbade her from seeming to flee from Hawke. She walked out on one of the docks, where the roof and the moored crafts concealed her from the far end of the marina, thinking that it was probably Laurie's presence that had kept Hawke here for so long. Certainly the business of stealing their marina could not have taken this much time. Why had this not occurred to her when she was so foolishly thinking Hawke was falling in love with her? Suddenly she knew why she had not gone home before now, why she had lingered here far longer than necessary: she had to say something to him to help dispel the rage that churned in her, had to tell him what she thought of him even though there was no hope of it changing anything. It might gain her nothing, but at least she would feel better for having said it, and it would end their relationship – not with the tenderness she had felt for him that night in the parlor – but with the bitterness it deserved.

Walking purposely back along the dock, she started slightly at the sight of Hawke on the gravel drive, not being aware that he had already left the *Pandora*. He stood quietly watching her, obviously waiting for her.

"I thought I saw you hiding in there," he said as she drew near.

"I wasn't hiding," she told him angrily, knowing that that had been her original purpose in walking out on the dock.

"Well, if you say so."

They had not spoken all week and looking at Hawke, Kimberly felt that he was a stranger, a hateful stranger who had somehow ensnared her emotions against her own will. Facing him now, she could almost hope that his coolly impersonal expression would change, and she would see again the caressing look that had been in his eyes when he had last held her in his arms. But it would mean nothing, she told herself; it would be as deceitful now as it had been then, and if he had already bought the mortgage, there was no longer any need for him to lull her suspicions.

"I was waiting for you," she told him. "Barry told me you bought the Side Wheel."

His eyebrows rose questioningly, but he said nothing, merely waiting for her to continue.

"And did you buy the mortgage on the marina too?" she finally asked.

"Yes."

He did not even have the grace to be ashamed of himself, she thought, staring at him with stormy eyes.

"You're a skunk," she finally said inadequately, all the things she wanted to call him lost in her overwhelming despair.

He laughed, throwing his head back in the way he did when he was hugely amused, his eyes alight with pleasure.

"Things have changed slightly now," he finally said. "And you're probably more anxious than ever to have the marina. I thought we might be able to come to some kind of an arrangement."

Kimberly stared at him in shocked disbelief. Despite the past, and the selfishness and brutality of which she knew he was capable, she had been lulled by her more recent contacts with him into forgetting the night he had made this same suggestion in her own parlor. He had not changed; she had merely been deceived.

Now she stared at him wordlessly, hating him and feeling at the same time a deep self-disdain for being able to love a man like this. There was still the shadow of a smile on his face as he stepped toward her, his hands reaching for her shoulders. She spun away from him, feeling a need to flee before her choking anger burst forth in tears. But there was nowhere to run except to the end of the dock, a futile, dead-end retreat. Then seeing her outboard, she leaped into it so swiftly that it rocked crazily in the slip and threatened to dump her into the harbor. Hawke reached for her, his smile changed now to a frown, but the swaying boat and her own efforts to right herself caused him to miss. With a quick snatch Kimberly loosed the rope that tied the boat, at the same time shoving at the dock with her other hand. And as the boat drifted slowly out of the slip, she started the motor. Almost blinded by tears, she brought the speed up quickly, too quickly for the sharp turn she had to make around the Side Wheel and then through the narrow opening into the river, almost capsizing the outboard in the attempt. But with quick skill she brought the boat straight and headed across the broad expanse of river, neither knowing nor caring where she was going.

Hawke's laughing face was clear in her mind's eye, and conflicting feelings of love and hate tore at her. She had lost everything: Richard was crippled; the marina was gone; and Hawke, whom she never had anyway, was a constant ache in her heart.

It was dusk but Kimberly had not thought of running lights, and between the tears raining down her face and her own distraught emotions, she neither saw nor heard the large cruiser that tried to swerve to miss her. She was aware only of the sharp crashing sound as it plowed into her broadside, the dreadful jolt, and then the weightless feeling as she and parts of the outboard flew into the air, arced, and landed in the water with a splash.

She went down, the water closing over her bringing panic as she tried to swim toward the surface. But something was wrong with her right knee; both pain and numbness made it almost impossible to move. And then she felt the pull of the undertow sweeping her along. Her lungs bursting, she fought upward, moving along with the current but ever reaching upward. After what seemed like an eternity, she came to the surface, gasping great drafts of air before she was dragged down again. This time she almost despaired of being able to reach the surface, when suddenly she felt herself released from the dragging undertow. Weakly, with senses reeling, knowing that despite herself she would soon be forced to breathe, and take in water, she strained her arms to move, and then, when it seemed all hope was gone and contained panic was mounting in her, she felt sand beneath her dragging right leg.

With her feet under her but barely able to stand, Kimberly leaned into the water for support as she took air into her burning lungs, choked, and then gasped again. Through drowned eyes she peered into the dimness and saw that she was in the lee of an island, ahead of her the young water lilies spreading their still immature leaves in a wide bed. With the last of her breath she waded toward these shallows, finally falling among the lily pads before she reached dry land. She lay there weakly, propped on her elbows to keep her head above the shallow water, her stentorian breathing slowly easing. But even when she was finally breathing in long, slow, regular gasps, she had no strength to move. Darkness was closing in when she finally attempted a slow crawl toward the island, her right knee shooting pain through her leg when she moved it. Inch by slow inch, she dragged herself forward until she reached the shore, and there, with her body still in the water and her head resting on her folded hands, she collapsed, falling into a comalike sleep.

It could have been hours or only minutes later when Kimberly finally lifted her head. For long, disoriented moments she gazed across the weedy sand so close to her face, unaware of where she was and not even alert enough to wonder. Something had awakened her, she felt, but that, too, was part of the vast, disinterested blankness that engulfed her. And then a light coming from behind bathed the sand and trees in brilliance, focusing directly on her. With a rush of awareness she recalled the shattering boat beneath her, her terrible fight with the river, and her exhausting crawl through the lily pads. There was the sound of a motor too. It had been there all the time, she suddenly realized, but it had somehow not penetrated her consciousness.

It came closer, the motor suddenly stopping, and then there were running footsteps through the shallow water behind her. Hawke was leaning close to her, his face in the light drawn and tense with an anguished expression Kimberly had never before seen there.

"Kimberly, are you hurt?" There was a gruff breathlessness in his voice.

"I don't think so," she tried to say, but her voice came so weakly that he had to lean closer to hear her. "I don't think so," she repeated in a stronger voice.

He was turning her, his hands gentle on her shoulders, his arm supporting her in the shallow water.

"Are you certain you're not hurt?"

"Something happened to my knee, but that's all. I just almost drowned."

His breath came in a ragged sigh as he drew her close, holding her in his arms while the numbness of shock slowly lifted from Kimberly's mind. With new awareness she recalled the reasons for her mad flight, and with weak hands she tried to push away from him. But his encircling arms tightened as he lifted his head and looked down into her face. Their eyes held for long moments and then his lips were warm on her cold face, his hand brushing back her wet hair.

At first Kimberly tried to resist. She tried futilely to turn her head, but he lifted his arm, holding her cradled and imprisoned as his dark head bent above her, his breath

235

short and sharp as he looked again into her face. A terrible weakness, reminiscent of her helplessness in the grip of the undertow, swept over her. She lay helpless in his arms, her hands clutching his shirt, unable to drag her gaze away from the fierce, hot light in his eyes.

"I thought I could leave you," he said in a strained voice. "I thought I could buy the marina for you and just walk away, but I can't."

Kimberly stared numbly at him. It was miracle enough that she had escaped from the river, but to hear these words from Hawke made her doubt her senses. Nothing seemed real – the sandy beach, the glare of the boat's spotlight amid the surrounding blackness of the night, her own helpless confusion, the memory of her terror as she fought the undertow of the river – and now Hawke, holding her in his arms and saying unbelievable things that she must have misunderstood. A tremor ran through her.

"I have to get you back," Hawke said suddenly. "Which knee is hurt?"

Kimberly told him, and he lifted her gently in his arms.

"I can walk," she said, not at all certain that she could.

Hawke ignored her protest, carried her

236

to the outboard he had run aground, and carefully eased her down into the seat.

As he sped back to the marina, Kimberly hesitantly flexed her knee. There was pain, but she could bend it and so tried again, assuring herself that nothing was broken. But when they reached the dock, she allowed the worried Mr. Glass and Hawke to lift her from the boat.

"I'm going to take her to the hospital," Hawke told Mr. Glass. "Will you signal the others that she has been found?"

"Are you hurt bad, Miss Cartwright?" Mr. Glass asked, concern in his face.

"No, I just hurt my knee. I don't think I have to go to the hospital."

Mr. Glass's eyes went to Hawke's face, a questioning look in them.

"She's going to the hospital," Hawke said with finality, lifting her again in his arms and moving toward the parking lot.

As they sped down the highway a feeling of euphoria enveloped Kimberly. Despite her injured knee she was alive and that was enough for the moment. Even the memory of Hawke's insult on the dock was of little importance, and, if not forgotten, then at least forgiven in her thankfulness at being alive.

Kimberly awoke early the next morning, gazing blankly at the hospital room for long moments before memory flooded back. Whatever they had given her the night before had plunged her into a deep restful sleep, undisturbed by the ache in her sprained knee that throbbed now with her first movement. In the hall she could hear the busy early-morning activity of the hospital – the rattle of dishes, the thump of breakfast trays, and the voices of the nurses – but Kimberly's thoughts were on the night before. The horror was gone from the memory now, as was the weakness of shock and exposure. She could recall her desperate fear as she fought the dragging water, her injured leg a useless weight, her lungs bursting for lack of air; but those moments on the beach with Hawke filled her thoughts. Impossible as it was to imagine his saying he could not leave her, she knew he *had* said it. She could hear his voice saying, "I thought I could buy the marina for you and just walk away, but I can't." A thrill of hope shot through her.

Then, almost as if she had summoned him with her thoughts, Hawke stood in the doorway. Her breath caught at the sight of him, and her heart seemed to beat in irregular violent bursts. His black hair was slightly rumpled, and his copper-tan face looked dark against the whiteness of his shirt. Just looking at him made something seem to melt and run inside her chest, suffusing her wildly beating heart. He stood lightly on his feet as if about to move, and he watched her, his eyes on her face seeming to search for something, but his own face was impassive, and Kimberly could read nothing in his expression.

"Hello, Hawke," she finally whispered into the long silence.

"They said you had a good night." He moved toward the bed as he spoke. "Are you feeling all right?"

"Yes, I'm fine," she told him, pressing the button that raised the head of the bed so that she was sitting up and better able to see him.

"Then you're feeling well enough to talk?" He moved to the bed and sat on its edge.

Confusion mounted in Kimberly. Moments before she had been certain he loved her. What else could he have meant when he said he could not leave her? But now he looked very cool; there was something almost calculating in his dark eyes and a grimness about his mouth.

"You should never have run away from me last night," he finally said, and Kimberly stared at him resentfully. He was talking about a time she would rather forget.

239

"You were well off. I bought the marina for you."

"You said something about that," she said uncertainly, not able to understand what he was telling her.

His lips pulled into a wry, humorless grin. "Yes, Kimberly," he said. "For the first time in my life I was almost gallant; I wasn't going to take what I wanted."

Her mouth curved into a smile as sudden realization dawned on her: he wanted her, he loved her. But he was going to buy the marina and leave without ever telling her. Why? she wondered. But it mattered little. All that mattered was that he loved her, and whatever it was he was trying to say was unimportant beside this one vital fact.

Suddenly his hands were on her shoulders, lifting her, and there was anger in his face. "Is that smile supposed to be a thank you for the marina? If it is, it isn't enough." There was a fierceness in the way his arms went around her, straining her to him as his dark head bent over her, his lips covering her mouth in a long, passionate kiss. Kimberly came alive in his arms, no longer fearful of her own wild emotions.

His breath was ragged when he lifted his head to look again into her face. "That isn't

240

enough either, Kimberly," he said with quiet anger. "I'll tell you the way it's going to be. You can have the marina, but you'll have to take me too." He shook her slightly. "Do you understand what I'm saying? You'll marry me, and the marina will be yours. And if we're very lucky, you might learn to love me."

"I don't have to learn to love you," she told him, tears of happiness streaming down her face.

He was suddenly rigid, holding her away from him, peering into her face, looking so unbelieving that she had to laugh through her tears.

"You mean . . . ?"

"I mean I've always loved you, Hawke. When you thought I only wanted to keep the marina, it was only you. And when you thought I was just passionate and easily aroused, it was only you."

For long moments he merely stared at her and then with a sigh he drew her close. Holding her tenderly, he rained kisses on her wet face. Kimberly nestled in his arms, her mind suffused with happiness, her thoughts involved only with Hawke, until a sudden awareness of the outside world intruded on her happy musings, and she suddenly sat up straight.

"Hawke, I can't leave my father!" she told him with sudden agitation.

But he forced her head back to his shoulder. "You don't have to leave your father," he told her. "If you don't invite me to live in your house, I'll buy another one in Elsah; I can't think of anyplace I'd rather live."

Kimberly relaxed again and there was silence between them until Hawke finally asked, his lips close to her ear, "Do you think you could ever learn to call me Chris?"